THAT PAIN IN THE WOMB

TALES OF ANGST AND HOPE

ASHA IYER KUMAR

Made with ♥ on the Notion Press Platform
www.notionpress.com

To

KṚṢṆA

who writes for me.

Contents

CHAPTER ONE

Return of the Spring

The last of our friends has just left. This was the first gathering we have had in almost a year. The scent of incense is still thick in the air. For many months now, all our prayer meetings have been virtual, and despite our best efforts to create a pious setting online, it somehow didn't equal the experience of a physical meeting.

I am deeply content that the chants we rendered together on this first day of the New Year spilled sacred vibes in the house and sought to exorcise the grim memories of the past. It makes me believe that the worst is now behind us in every respect, for our family and the world at large.

I begin to put away the dishes into the sink humming the last bhajan we sang that evening when the phone buzzes. I wipe my hands hurriedly on my saree.

It's a good night message from Tanu. I was too preoccupied during the day to call her and honestly, amidst all the chores I had forgotten to even think of her. I feel a sudden stab of remorse. It is needless, but real.

'Hp d evng wnt wel, Ma. Hw mny ppl cme?'

I see that she is still typing, and I wait for her to finish before writing a reply.

'Ma, Im cmg thr tmrw 2 b wid u fr som time. May b a few mnths.'

My first impulse was to type a 'why', but I stop myself

in time. What an absurd question to ask a daughter eager to come home and spend time with her mother!

The house has felt desolate ever since she left. Although she was little more than a shadow lurking around us when she was here, that shadows can also fill empty spaces amply was testified when her absence began to bite us. The news of her visit should only have made my heart leap with delight, but it did not.

It set the alarm bells in my head ringing.

I gulp my rising panic, gather my wits, and type the words with dreadful anticipation as I keenly sense something amiss. 'Id ervythnig OK?'

I don't bother to correct the typos. 'Hmm...OK.'

'What is it, Tanu? Why suddenly coming and staying with us?' I give up and eventually ask her straight.

'Nthng Ma. Wl tel u tmrw whn I cm. Im gng 2 slp nw.Gn8.'

I am tempted to call her at once but I let it be. What if her husband is with her and he doesn't appreciate it? She is new in that family, barely three months old. Life must be still striving to get into the groove and I realise that it isn't like when she went to her husband's house the first time.

Tanu was a bouncy young girl then: dreamy-eyed and happy to fall in love. She was eager to enter the wedlock, impatient to start a family, and be 'the happiest woman in the world'. That was how she envisaged herself in life.

I had often wondered during the initial days of her marriage if we weren't a bit hasty in dispatching her into domesticity. In these times, twenty-one years is unusually early for a girl to be married, albeit of her own volition. She had taken an instant liking to the Shankars' son when they came visiting, and when they later broached the subject of his alliance with Tanu, she gladly accepted it.

Her consent was a pleasant surprise to her father and me. That a girl who at one point in time had wanted to be an independent career woman was now wholeheartedly accepting a totally different offer from destiny amused us. She was over the moon, proudly announcing to her friends that post wedding she would relocate to Paris, the city of love.

How instantly girls can fall in love with their fiancés! Someone who had been a complete stranger turns into a hallowed hero the moment a nuptial agreement is made by the parents! I tried to think if things were the same when my wedding was fixed twenty-eight years ago. No, I was more apprehensive than excited; falling in love wasn't even on the charts for me. To be a good wife and daughter-in-law, to raise a happy family, to learn new cuisines, to be good at housekeeping, these were the things I was told to concentrate on. Of course, by the time Tanu's turn came, things had changed. Romance preceded everything and girls made no bones about revealing their sentiments. Tanu didn't even pretend to hide her smitten state from me.

I still remember her impish smile when I caught her chatting on the phone in the middle of the night.How happy my little doll had been! How pleased was I to see her glowing in her newfound love, despite my secret pain of having to see her fly away to another country!

'I am both happy and sad,' I said, wiping a stealthy tear on his shoulder a day before the wedding.

'That's how every parent feels when they hand their daughter over to someone. These are times when girls test their parents' patience by laying down conditions of all kinds before agreeing to an alliance, and Tanu has spared us of all those woes. We are blessed.'

I couldn't agree more to what he said. Only, our agreement or disagreement had no sanctity in fate's real estate. It made devious plans behind our backs, and waited in ambush, ready to slay us.

With Tanu's message still playing on my mind, I turn the kitchen lights off and go to our room. Tanu's father is preparing to sleep. I pause for a moment in front of him toying with my phone, debating with myself if I must share Tanu's message with him. I decide that I must, for my own sanity. Otherwise, the night would be a baleful stretch, hauling me over my invented fears.

'Tanu is coming tomorrow,' I say carefully, making sure that my anxiety doesn't show through.

'Did she call you? I had wanted to speak to her too. My phone hasn't been behaving since yesterday and I haven't been able to post anything on Facebook. I want to ask her what needs to be done to fix it.'

I am slightly irked that while my mind is roiling in forbidden thoughts and imagined fear, he is lost in his world of Facebook posts. I can't blame him. He is relishing this freedom and peace after a long time. Three and half years to be precise. It is only in the three months since Tanu left for her husband's house that he has taken to pastimes like writing and posting poetry on Facebook, hunting down bees and butterflies in the garden to click, and reading translated versions of classic novels.

'No, she didn't call. Just sent a message. She said she is coming tomorrow...to be with us for some days. Or even months.' I deliberately drag the last part of the sentence to stress my discomfort.

He still doesn't sense my disquiet. He doesn't seem overly concerned that she has made a sudden decision to come and stay with us. Fathers often don't see a calamity even when it is apparent. Mothers can smell it from a mile. The womb has a sixth sense that speaks like a soothsayer. I don't wait further and spit out my fear.

'Do you think something might be wrong there?' I can't spell out what the 'something' can be. I can't imagine what can go wrong. Again.

Tanu's father briefly turns from where he stood fiddling with his malfunctioning phone and throws me a piqued glare. I hope to see some trace of alarm in his eyes too, but there is none.

'What could be wrong? You are paranoid, Rema. Whatever had to happen has happened. It's all over. Don't let the memories of the past cast a shadow on her life, our lives.'

'How can you get over it? I just can't. It still gives me panic attacks. It still jolts me from sleep. How did you get over it? Please, tell me!' I cried.

From the sight of the coffin being brought out of the airport, to Tanu's frozen zombie-like state for weeks after that, to her abrupt attempt to quit life, and when it failed, her decision to join the ashram—I could not get over anything.

Each frame of the cursed past flashes before my eyes as I read Tanu's message again.

'There is something not right there,' I repeat. 'Stop it, Rema. You are over-thinking.'

'No, I am not. I am thinking like a mother with all her latent fears coming out. I am thinking like a mother whose memories are filled with her only daughter's early widowhood. I am thinking like a mother whose every moment is spent in the worry of her daughter's new life. You won't understand. You just won't understand.'

Tanu's father says nothing and lets me vent my distress. He knows the only way I can unburden myself is by ranting aloud.

'Now, quiet...quiet. Enough, or you will fall sick again,' he says after a full ten minutes of my raving and hands me half a tablet of Remeron and a glass of water.

'Now lie down and listen to a story,' he says, rubbing my back.

I knew it was coming. It was the only remedy to my meltdowns. Together with the pill, it put me to sleep, taking me far from the day when our world had come apart without any prior notice.

I often caught only snatches of what he said, but as I cruised into sleep, I knew that this story was a happy one. It was a tale of good things and a happy ending. I found huge comfort in that conviction.

'You know, my dear wife, life is fair for most parts,' he begins. 'But sometimes it goes crazy, as if bitten by a dog. That's when tragedies happen. But there is someone who cures life of its madness and puts things back in their place. Not in the way we ask, but in a way that keeps life going on.'

I smile at this point and whisper, 'God.' An evening bhajan emerges in my partly awake consciousness and I hum under my breath.

The story then takes me through images of Tanu and a man in his mid-thirties, dressed in simple wedding costumes standing in front of the deity.

It wasn't easy to get her to agree. The five years she had spent in Paris were too deeply etched in her memory.

Forgetting her first love and accepting someone new in her life was much the same as infidelity to her.

'I am not capable of loving anyone again,' she had said, categorically. 'If you force me, I will join the Brahmakumaris,' she had threatened.

How does a mother tolerate such pronouncements from her young daughter? For three and a half years, her heart lay in splinters on which she walked barefoot, her soul bleeding from all ends.

'Sometimes miracles happen faster than maladies,' I hear Tanu's father say.

This is my favourite sentence in the story. I smile once again through my pill-induced drowsiness. Tanu's father has a unique way of accenting that sentence for me. The way he intones it, it obliterates all the pains of the past and puts hope and happiness in sharp relief.

From here on, the story gallops fast. Most of what he says glide past me but even in my semi-conscious state I know what he is saying. As he describes the scene of a couple exchanging rings and garlands in front of the deity, I faintly picture it in my mind.

The young woman is standing in nervous anticipation. Her eyes are glistening. It is hard to say what they reflected. The priest emerges from the sanctum, hands over the mangalsutra to the man, and instructs him to tie it around the young woman's neck. He then indicates him to follow it by smearing the red vermillion in her hair parting.

My Tanu is a bride again, resplendent in my pink Benarasi saree. She had insisted on wearing it for this occasion. It was auspicious, and it will protect her from future harm, she said.

The One who fixes things that are broken had got her to consent to a second chance. She was smiling again. She had allowed herself to love someone again. She had agreed to try and release herself from the clutches of a tragic past.

The prayer meeting in the evening was organised to give the Fixer of things a big thanks for sowing happiness in our lives again. At that thought, I must have fallen asleep, for the next thing I remember is waking up in the morning to the beep of my mobile phone.

The fairy tale had dissipated somewhere in the darkness and the queasiness of last night made an instant come back. I pat around the bedside table urgently for my glasses and the phone.

Tanu's father is still asleep. For a moment, I consider waking him up to read the message. I don't have the courage to do it myself. I am desperate with dismal thoughts.

What if something untoward had happened in Tanu's new house? What if she was in distress? What if...? What if...?

I sit up in the bed, hold my breath and brace for whatever news the message had to bring.

'Ma', it reads.

'Papa snt me a msg lst nt abt d txt I hd snt u yday abt cmg hme. He sd u hd pnickd a lot thnkg smthg ws wrng & he wntd me 2 snd u a msg 1st thng in d mrng. Ma, I'm cmng home 2 b wid u & Papa 4 sm dez. U may wnt 2 kno y.

Ma, u r gng 2 b a grandma! & d doc hs advsed rst.

I wntd to gv u a srprse whn I cm hom 2day, bt papa sd u wr 2 tense lst nt. Sry ma, 4 csng panic. I wil c u in d evng. Lv u lots.'

Can this be true? I read the message again and again to ascertain its truth. I shake Tanu's father awake. This time I was frantic with joy.

'Listen, Tanu is pregnant. Tanu is pregnant,' I exult through my tears. 'And what all terrible things I had imagined, oh God!'

Tanu's father opens his eyes fleetingly, shakes his head, smiles and mumbles, 'Crazy woman,' before pulling up the blanket and slipping into an extended snooze.

I heave with relief and for the first time in a long while, I give him a tight hug (over the blanket), plant a kiss on his forehead and scamper to the prayer room.

Later, as the morning rays seep in through the windows, and fills our house with a delightful glow, I make a video call to Tanu.

'Hello, beta...' I say, and softly kiss the screen.

CHAPTER TWO

The Gift of Petrichor

'Da-daaam! That's how it all began,' Budha Baba said with an overwhelming authority in his voice. Old and shrivelling, he sat cross-legged with his white sarong scrunched up to his knees, revealing his spindly legs from which ripened veins protruded in branches and knots. He could have easily been two to three hundred years old.

It was the weekly story-telling night in the village. The elders of the community took turns to narrate stories drawn from the past to the little boys and girls who had yet to know the vagaries of life. This particular night, it was a full house with even the adults in attendance. No one wanted to miss the stories that Budha Baba brought from the places he had passed through the centuries.

Budha Baba did not belong to the village. It wasn't even his real name. He had come from somewhere, at some point in time, but did not live in their midst. It took a long time for them to accept him into their fold, mainly because he looked strange and spoke of weird things. No one asked him anything because he generally didn't like questions and dismissed all those who asked him anything with a lancing glare. He came to the village gathering only once in a month. Where he lived at other times, no one knew.

When they asked him his name, he said he had none.

So, they simply gave him a name by consensus.

Budha Baba. The old man.

The villagers did not particularly have a liking for him given his snappish nature, but when he was around, a sweet scent permeated the air which soothed their disturbed minds. He told surreal stories when he came visiting on full moon nights. For this, they turned up in huge numbers—boys and girls, men and women.

That night he had a macabre tale to tell. He said that he had witnessed the end of the world in his childhood, and that God had appeared before him and had said with a wave of His hand, 'You are the only one I am sparing. The rest will all die. And when I ordain, you will rebuild the world for me.' That was how the world had come to be all over again—by dint of his efforts, he bragged.

It was all too grand and outlandish for the people in the village to take in, and at least some of them suspected he was concocting the tales just to beguile them. Yet, they listened to him with great intrigue because his stories helped them beat life's big and small annoyances and produced fantastic dreams in their sleep.

That night when he mentioned God in his tale, they shook the tedium of yet another long, laborious day and sat in rapt attention. They had heard of God, but had no inkling of what He was like – to look, feel or know.

'How does God look?' Ten-year-old Chaamu who sat squeezed between his parents chewing his nails, wanted to know. Like most in his clan, he had never prayed, never asked for benediction, never known God.

Budha Baba squinted his eyes and peered in the direction of the question to make sure that there was no ridicule concealed in it. If there was as much as a slight snigger that came with the question, he would abandon his story and walk away into the night and be gone, not to be seen until the next full moon.

How many stories had he left unfinished that way? No one in the village wanted to go to sleep with an unfinished story wobbling in their head. It gave them molten sleep in which they had frightful dreams.

'Why, like me! God looked like me,' Budha Baba said, casually. His manner of saying made it nearly sound like he himself was God.

Chaamu blinked incredulously and before he could ask anything further, the snot from his perennially running nose dribbled down, and tickled by it, he sneezed.

'Achooo!'

The crowd held its breath wondering if the random, unintended response from Chaamu might offend the old man to hobble away leaving the story midway. The past weeks had been restless and sleep had evaded them for a while as if a curse had befallen them. The only thing that could placate their nerves was Budha Baba's scented presence and they badly wanted him in their midst that full moon night.

Mosquitoes whined night songs into their ears and feasted on their blood as the post-sneeze moments passed by. Chaamu's father whacked a tiny vampire that landed on his son's cheek, and the crowd took it to be a punitive act for the untimely disruption that the boy had caused and nodded in approval. The punishment was in place.

Just as the boy began to moan, Budha Baba raised his hand theatrically, and struck the air in front of him hard.

'Da-daam!' he thundered.

The loudness of his voice implied that the story had resumed and silence had to prevail. Ears perked up and Chaamu's father silenced his son by cupping his palm over his snot-washed mouth.

'It was as if the sky had crashed down and broken into splinters. And then water began to fall from all sides of the roof. There was no hole, no gap between the tiles; yet the water came down, first in small drips and then in huge gushes. It was as if we were sitting under an open, pouring sky. We had never seen so much water in our lives. It had the colour of rust. It was hot. And toxic. It scorched everything it fell on.'

The crowd, on tenterhooks, stiffened as Budha Baba recalled that night of horror.

'I took cover under the table and saw my parents' legs dissolving in the deluge as they scurried for dry ground and found none. And slowly as I watched, the things in the house fell and began to liquefy. I screamed at the top of my lungs as I saw the waters slowly consume them. At one point, I saw four eyes floating in front of me, and then they were gone too. As the water level began to rise, I ran on my burning feet and climbed into an empty iron chest in the attic and shut myself in. My siblings were asleep in the other room, and I do not know what became of them. The orange waters must have eaten them up too.'

The old men and women in the crowd stared at Budha Baba through their hazy cataracts, trying to imagine what the orange waters coming down from the skies might have been like. A few among the young looked askance, unimpressed by the tale.

'Water can never fall from the skies,' one of them averred and his friends agreed. They had never witnessed rain in all their lives.

'It used to, in those days. When I was a little boy, water used to fall from the sky. In two seasons, in precise patterns, as if it had an agreement with nature.' Budha Baba closed his eyes as if to summon memories of what was once called a 'monsoon.'

The lines on his wizened face glistened in the wan streetlights as he spoke of a time when, as a boy, he had floated paper boats in the courtyard of his house with his siblings.

'Everyone knew exactly when the rains would come and how many months they would stay. It was like a guest that brought happiness in our lives. Our fields were fed and our grains grew. There was no dearth.'

Nostalgia rippled in his voice as his memory rolled backwards. It unfurled, revealing a whole new world to the villagers who sucked their tongues in awe when he said that the wells and pond used to be so full that they could draw water by hand and drink whenever they wanted. The fields were verdant and endlessly generous. And what's more, they breathed directly from nature.

Unlike now when they drew air through pipes from the cylinders tied around their waist.

The villagers waved him off with disbelief. A loud yawn from someone set off a wave of yawns among the crowd but they refused to budge from where they sat. The old man was weirder than they thought, but what he spoke was intriguing. Some of them dismissed it as fiction while the others insisted on having more of it. Somewhere back in time, it seemed life was in perfect sync. There was water for the asking, people breathed from nature, the fields were bountiful, no one died for want of food or air. These were things they couldn't conjure up in their dreams even on full moon nights.

'Is there a way for us to get back to those times?' Chaamu's father stood up and asked eagerly, making no effort to hide his wonder. The men and women around him were pleased that he had asked it and chorused after him.

'Is there? Is there?'

Just then a deep moan rose from the crowd. A woman had just run out of her oxygen and died even as she was listening to Budha Baba's tale. People tried to shake her back to life, but she was dead beyond any chance of revival. The woman was middle-aged and lived alone after she had lost her children and husband to a strange fever that had swept the village two years ago.

'Good. It is one less misery for us to put up with,' Chaamu's father said. He pulled the pipe from the woman's nostrils as if it were a creeper climbing on a tree, and tossed the empty can out. He and a few others lifted the woman's body and took it away.

There was an acute shortage of oxygen cylinders in recent times and people even resorted to stealing whenever they ran short. It was considered legal. No one could be prosecuted for finding means to procure urgent aids for survival. Fights broke out at the slightest instance and people could kill for a can of clean air or an ounce of pure water. Blood was spilled as indiscriminately as water was drained in earlier times. There was scant regard for the red fluid that ran in their veins, and that was an irony in itself. What they attempted to sustain was what they let flow so recklessly on the streets.

The brief stir in the atmosphere caused by the woman's death settled with a few murmurs of pity. It was a routine affair. Someone or the other kept dying for want of air.

A man with two cylinders ostensibly tied around his waist urged Budha Baba to continue with his story. He was a crafty businessman and a hoarder of things, but no one raised a finger or uttered a word against him. No one risked getting crushed by his material power. The ones who could buy and hoard the resources, did so. Those who couldn't, died quietly. Money and might was life. It was as simple as that.

'Don't waste time over the dead. She was of no use to us, anyway,' the rich man said in his haughty voice alluding to the woman. 'Tell us more about the Da-daam night. What happened thereafter?' he urged.

'As I said, I shut myself up in the iron box. It was dark inside and it stank of mouldering grain. It was where all the wheat that was produced in my father's fields used to be stored. For many months though, it had lain empty. Our land had become fallow, you see. It hadn't rained for three years and all our stocks were getting depleted. We first used to eat thrice a day, and then twice. In the days before the big Da-daam, we ate only once, that too frugally.

I passed out inside the chest. For the first time I knew what it felt like to be choked; to be without air to breathe. But God was merciful. There was a breach in the box that allowed air inside, and it kept me alive. Curled up like a foetus, how long I must have remained there, I don't know.

Between short spells of wakefulness and long periods of sleep, I had cataclysmic dreams. And somewhere amidst it, God made an appearance. I was eager to know what had happened outside, what had become of my family and my village. And what in his holy name it was all about.'

'How did you know it was God?' a young man probed from the far end of the gathering.

'He said so, and I believed.' Budha Baba didn't feel it was necessary to explain.

'That was daft, to believe someone who called himself God,' declared another young man as he rose to leave because the story wasn't going anywhere. Moreover, he had to get his air ration early in the morning. He would have to bribe the man at the air station for a few extra canisters. His lungs had been more demanding of late and he had not been able to provide for them amply. His coughs were getting worse by the day. At this rate, he couldn't expect to live beyond a few months.

'Yes, daft,' affirmed Budha Baba. 'That's what God said to me too. That we were all downright daft. Foolish to the last cell in our bodies. And for our foolishness, He said, we would pay. Our sufferings had just begun. The Dadaam was only a sign. The worst was yet to come upon our children, their children and theirs, until one day when this whole place would freeze to a deathly silence.'

He paused, gave the gathering and the space beyond it a sweeping glance. He then inhaled deeply and pronounced, 'The end is imminent.'

There was a grave sense of foreboding in Budha Baba's voice that dragged the young man back to his seat. He tried to swallow his panic and regain calm. For in the moments when his heart beat spiked, the amount of oxygen that he spent increased too. He could not afford that, not in these times of shortage. He had to conserve his resources.

'Whose end?' he managed to ask with dread.

'Yours. Yours. Yours. And yours,' said the old man, pointing randomly at people from one end to the other. 'The end of everyone and everything.'

The men and women winced at the prophecy. The flutter in their heart became too loud to contain within their body. They began to wheeze in the bluster of the winds that blew across the empty swathes of land that were once decked in winding rivers and wild roses.

They couldn't perish so easily. They hadn't done anything so gross to deserve it, they averred to each other. Their eyes began to well up with fear and they hurried to collect the falling tears in little crucibles that they carried with them. It was water, after all. Every droplet of sweat, tears, and urine was valuable. They sent it to the factories and it came back as water.

'Tell us more. Tell us more,' they chanted. Some wrapped their arms around their body as if to protect themselves from an impending catastrophe.

'It isn't your fault entirely. You are merely reaping the rotten fruits of what people in my time and before that did out of greed. Although, I must add that you have done nothing better to reverse it.' Budha Baba grunted as if to emphasise.

'That night God spoke to me about wicked human exploits that I hadn't heard of in my ten years of life. Men had drilled holes in the skies with their goddamn guns and planes. They had splashed poison in the skies and seas. They had shoved trash into the fishes' gullets and filled the earth's gut with filth. There was a deluge after years of drought in our district, but elsewhere, there were deadly infernos. Fire and water, water and fire, everywhere.

The Da-daam that fell on us that night wasn't a normal occurrence. It wasn't a simple bolt of thunder that came with our monsoons. It was pure wrath of the universe. The red rain didn't pour on us for nothing. My parents and thousands of others dissolved in the acid rain because of human depravity,' he ranted.

After a brief pause, he shook his head and declared, 'It wasn't you; it was them. They sapped life out of existence.'

'Who?' The question that came was barely a whisper. 'Those damned wolves. The people of my time. Your selfish ancestors.'

As he spoke, the sand dunes in the sprawling desert behind them shifted with discomfort. The night air began to grow colder and the crowd began to shiver. They thought of their ancestors with utter despise. They spat and hurled abuses in their head. Pity, that the dead can't be castigated with anything worse than hateful thought.

'Will there be a Da-daam night again? Here?' Chaamu tossed a wary question from behind his mother's podgy frame. His father had yet to return from wherever he had gone to dump the dead woman.

'Who knows? It could, anytime. The worst isn't over yet. One more Da-daam and...it's all over. Not even an ant will roam these streets after that,' Budha Baba said, indicating doom with a swish of his bony hands.

Stunned by his own forewarning, he stared at the ground for a few moments and then, firming his head up, threw a stern question at Chaamu. 'You are scared, aren't you?'

Chaamu nodded cagily.

'What are you afraid of?'

'Of dying,' came the answer from an anonymous corner.

No one cared to look who said it, but it spoke for all of them. They all harboured the same fear in their hearts. 'Of dying?' Budha Baba guffawed. 'To die one must first be alive. Who said you are alive? Ghosts. That's what you are. Shadows of existence. You call this futile lugging around of your body saddled with cylinders, living?'

He received blank stares in response. The stillness that enveloped them was sinister and scary. No one dared speak a word. The wind whooshed across the desert beyond them and kicked up the restive sand. There was a dust storm brewing in the arid expanse. They tasted it on their lips and felt it on their skin. Some even began to imagine the sky was gathering steam to orchestrate another Da-daam.

'I should have been dead too that night, but God spared me,' Budha Baba continued his narration amid the encircling gloom. 'He stopped the red rain from seeping into the iron chest. Do you know why?'

The swagger that he had displayed before when speaking of his encounter with God earlier was missing now. He had a new truth to reveal and it was so solemn that it required him to be unpretentious.

'Why?'

'Because I made a random promise to him...that in a few hundred years, I will restore everything that was wiped out. That I will atone for all the decadence of my generation. It was a promise I made on an impulse to save my life. I had no clue how I would keep it. How I would bring back all the riches the greedy pilferers robbed from this place, how I would keep generations alive despite it all, I didn't know. But I made the promise because I didn't want to die. Not for something I wasn't guilty of. I was, after all, a child. I didn't make the oceans deadly and the skies toxic. So why did I have to pay with my life?' He narrowed his eyes and asked.

The crowd nodded in agreement.

Although his voice was infinitesimally dismal, they were now beginning to see tiny slivers of hope in his words. If he could be spared to live a few hundred years by dint of a promise he had made to God, they could well live too. They hadn't done mean things to the sky and the sea and the earth. If something was to be blamed, it was the depravity of their forefathers. And now they had a chance to wash their old sins and start all over again. They had an obligation to help the old man keep his promise. For their own sake, and for those they wished to carry in their wombs in the future.

The murky moonlight descended on them in gauzy layers as if to bless their new intent. It made sure that the sanctity of the nocturnal hours remained intact even when everything else had become profane.

The men and women went into a sudden huddle as if they had a plan and whispered their thoughts amongst themselves in feverish tones. They still had a chance—to prevent the acid rain, to save themselves from liquefying out of existence. It was true that the wrongs people did in their lifetime came back to haunt their offspring.

One by one, the men, women and children fanned out of the huddle, held their palms together, took it close to their mouth, closed their eyes and whispered a promise

into it. They brought their hand to their chest, let it linger there for a while and then lifted it to their foreheads.

In the middle of this solemn ritual, Chaamu's father suddenly raised his head in Budha Baba's direction and asked, 'But where is God? We want to see God.'

Budha Baba stroked his snow-white beard that cascaded down and covered his ribbed chest. 'Tell me what you want from God,' he said, gravely.

'We want to make promises to Him. Like the one you made. We want to be saved from future Da-daams. Take us to God.'

'Yes, take us to God so that we can make promises too,' the others cried.

'I am His messenger. Give me your promises and I will take them to Him,' Budha Baba said, gently. 'Only if you are sure that you will keep them. Remember, promises to God without pure intent are blasphemous.' Chaamu's father scratched his head and considered Budha Baba's words. If it was true that he had seen God, then they were as close as they could get to seeing God himself. So, his words were gospels. They had no choice but to put their trust in his words and hand over the fate of their lives to him. He was their last resort.

That night, from being a mere raconteur, Budha Baba suddenly became their saviour.

Holding their promises tight in their fists, the villagers made a line toward the old man, their head bowed in deep reverence. The fear in their eyes had softened and it was replaced by a glint of faith and resolve. They crouched in front of him and laid their promises down. He gathered them with a sweep and thrust them into his rucksack.

The crowd—half in doubt, half in belief—held its breath, waiting for Budha Baba to offer them a word of assurance that all would be well henceforth. But he said nothing. Rising to his feet he walked into the dark and went out of sight. They watched him take their promises with him.

'What will he do with them? Discard them on his way or pass it on to God?' There was no way to know what was in store. Their faith alone could sustain them until he came back again.

The crowd began to disperse taking the sillage of his scent with them to soothe their aching souls. They felt a strange lightness come over their being like it had never before.

That night they all had a dream. A single dream in every pair of eyes in the village. Young and old alike.

A withered old man hobbled across a barren desert, scattering seed-like things from a rucksack. Where a seed landed, a drop of water fell from the sky. From there arose tiny green shoots, as if the desert had had goosebumps on its skin at the touch of the old man's feet. Not once did the man turn around to see the trail of magic he was leaving in his wake. He kept walking as if a task had at long last been completed and he had no reason to look back or return. He disappeared from the dream in the hours before dawn.

In the morning, the villagers woke up to a miracle.

It was raining outside. The kind of rain Budha Baba had described.

The water was colourless and it ran in tiny streams down the streets. Children floated paper boats in it and hopped in the puddles in their courtyards with mirth. Men and women came out and inhaled deeply as if it was their first breath of life.

There was a new fragrance in the air. Petrichor. The scent of promise emanating from the womb of the earth. Their special gift from God.

CHAPTER THREE

PAYBACK

Pappan gets out of the car and hands the keys to the valet, feeling privileged and satisfied in a way he has never before. For the first time ever, he has driven the Mercedes without his uniform, as if the car was his own. It felt different to not have Muthalali sitting behind, with his over-powering, imperious aspect breathing down the neck.

Muthalali was a man of abundant abuses.

Pappan deeply resented Muthalali's arrogant nature and he frequently entertained foolish ideas of bumping him off some way or the other, but he swallowed the recurring rancour thinking of his father who was Muthalali's original driver for decades before he died.

Muthalali took Pappan in as his driver almost as if it was the only way to be employed, despite his graduation degree. As though Pappan's family was pledged to Muthalali's life forever. It wasn't a thought he particularly relished, but today, he was a man on an important mission assigned by Muthalali. A task that he knew could have unimaginable consequences in their lives.

Pappan walks towards the lobby of the hotel with the confidence of a man who knew why exactly he was born and how to accomplish his goal. He nods at the usher at the door who has no suspicion of him whatsoever.

Inside, Pappan allows himself for a pat-down, something practices, he lets himself go through the procedures.

He looks around, unsure of which way to proceed.

'May I help you, sir?' A honeyed voice behind him queries.

Turning around, he sees a young woman's face framed in brown curls, flashing a smile that he has seen only in tooth paste advertisements. What strikes him immediately are the pink lipstick and an extraordinary pair of eyelashes. That a woman so beautiful would address him as 'sir' is inconceivable to him, and in his dazed state, he holds the invitation card out to her.

Vivek weds Sandhya.

'This way to the banquet hall, sir,' she says, showing him the way. He looks down a long, carpeted corridor, and quickly appraises the people around. Their unerring haughtiness grates on his skin and he shudders with disdain.

It is all surreal. This task he is on, this setting, this woman, and this festering nervousness. He feels like a hit man out on his first contract to kill, teetering between determination and doubt. With sweat threatening to break out from every pore in his body, he walks towards the banquet hall along with a waft of perfumes from people coasting down with him. He detests their affected presence and the feeling of meagreness they inadvertently leave in him as they pass by.

With stealth lining his eyes, he scans the area soaked in miscellaneous varieties of snobbery. He is looking for a girl, who does not know he exists, or the story that has brought him here. He has no reasons to be discreet but still he has to be careful. He is standing near the doorway and surveying the golden banquet hall, which is filled with refined bodies in saris and jackets, and beautiful young women with straight hair who never make facial expressions. But they will, soon. Any moment now.

He pulls out an envelope from his pocket, and walks towards a young woman with a tray of fried snack that had little sticks poked into them.

'Sir, chicken lollipops?' she asks as he approaches her. He picks one, surveying her face carefully. And before she moves away, he grabs her hand suddenly and the tray falls to the ground, scattering pieces of fried fowl on the carpet. All attention now gathers to where he stands, like iron dust to a magnet.

'I am sorry,' he says, as the look of horror on the woman's face freezes and she stands heaving. He is grateful to her for not raising an alarm.

'I am sorry, I didn't mean to. I just wanted you to give this envelope to the bride,' he says in an attempt to calm her and defuse the tension.

'It's...a gift cheque...from a friend who couldn't make it to the wedding,' he stammers to the perplexed woman. 'I am his driver.'

The woman doesn't seem convinced, but she takes the envelope warily and turns to go towards the bride. Unaware of what was happening at the other corner of the hall, the bride stands gushing beside her tall groom, her hennaed hands locked in his.

No one in the hall knew that she was faking her feelings. She was far from being in love with the man she was hitched with. She has nothing new to give this man. Her love, in all its physical and spiritual dimensions, has already been spent for another man who dumped her for his family. But she can pretend love for a lifetime and her husband will never catch wind of it. She knows it. What she does not know is what happened to the other man after they split unceremoniously. Theirs was an unequal love—love that often remains inconclusive.

In a moment of panic, Pappan turns to flee, his instincts wanting him to vanish before someone gets suspicious. He stops upon remembering Muthalali's stern words. 'Don't come without getting her.'

Wedding receptions are such tedious occasions, Sandhya thinks, fretfully. She can't wait for the evening to close and for the guests to leave. Not because she has anything to look forward to beyond it, but she is genuinely tired and all she wants is to plonk herself in the bed and sleep.

But life is on a cusp and the night will not end in a hurry.

Sandhya unlocks her hand with Vivek and moves towards a hostess for a soft drink. Pappan hopes that the woman with the envelope will use this opportunity for his errand, and much to his relief, she does. Sandhya opens the envelope with a calm befitting a bride.

Laden with anxiety, Pappan scratches the invitation card with his thumb nail and the embossed gilt on 'Vivek' begins to wear. Anything could have gone wrong with the plan, by now. The hostess whose hand Pappan grabbed could have created a scene and got him caught red-handed, she could have chosen a wrong moment to hand the envelope, or Sandhya could have passed the envelope to someone standing nearby without even opening it. It takes nothing for the best laid plans to go awry. However, against all odds, Sandhya opens it as though she is programmed for it, and pulls out the note nestling in it.

Jaan,

How can you get married when I am still waiting for you?

Mahesh.

With feet trembling under wobbly knees, Sandhya darts towards the woman who brought the message to her and together they look around as though trying to spot somebody. Her pounding heart threatens to tear her wedding finery and fall out in a lump. From the verge, it calls out a name it has never forgotten. MAHESH. The name could have clambered from the chamber of her heart to her mouth and spilled out any moment. She fights hard to not cry.

There is only a slender line that separates foolishness from naïveté. Disaster strikes when that line blurs and sets one up on a path to self-ruin. It often happens unconsciously, the impulse driving the disaster to finest of destinies can stop tragedy from happening.

Sandhya finds Pappan lingering near the door. Pappan looks at the unsettled bride now approaching

him. His uneasy but eager expression betrays his intention to sweep her out of the hall in a flash.

Pappan gears up for the moment. It is a moment that will settle a lot of things in his life too.

'Where is he?' Sandhya asks, her eyes exploding into countless flickers, each one reflecting an urgent question from her past, present and future.

'Come with me. He is waiting for you.'

'Who are you? And why should I believe what you are saying?'

Pappan opens the invitation cover, pulls a photograph out and flashes it in front of her. A moment from the past says peek-a-boo and quickly returns to its place inside the cover.

'That's you and him, isn't it? He gave it to me to show you as evidence. Now, come with me. Quietly. Before they notice your absence on the dais.'

Sandhya stands indecisively, unable to determine the veracity of Pappan's words. Even if it is true, what obligation does she have to return to an old love that she was forced to forget after Mahesh succumbed to his father's pressures like a spineless nincompoop?

Yes, there were the undeniable differences between them—of caste and class. She was the daughter of a low caste proletariat whose family had come into good money only after the land reforms. He had aristocracy tagged to his name which couldn't be rivalled by any amount of new-fangled fortune of hers. Why didn't he consider these factors before sending out his first missive of love for her in college? Didn't he know then? Why then wasn't he man enough to stand up to his father when he threatened to disown him and leave nothing of his wealth for him in his will?

Besides, if he chickened out then, why is he back crawling now? Is the man who threatened them with the words 'I will shoot you both dead' himself dead? Is Mahesh now free to take possession of her?

The lure of an old flame is irresistible, with the power to draw blinded night insects towards it and singe it in a seductive instant. It is hard to say if the insect is conscious of its folly and consigns itself to the flame as an act of supreme sacrifice in love or it is too guileless to think.

Then there is the guilt, of course, of having moved on with life when Mahesh was waiting all the while. But life gives a second chance, doesn't it? To squander it will be foolishness. She will go, regardless of what the rest of the crowd in the hall thinks of her. It isn't their life. After all, they do not face the prospect of sleeping with a man they don't love. She does. And now she has an opportunity to defy it. Sandhya feels an old pang arise and sting her mascara-fringed eyes.

'Wait somewhere between the entrance and the main gate till I get the car, and make sure no one spots you there. This wedding dress is dangerous,' Pappan hisses, angrily. He is now emboldened by the fact that the plan was working like a charm. He now has a firm control, both over the girl and the situation that was getting incredible with each passing minute.

Reeling under the rush of blood to his head, he goes to fetch the Mercedes that he imagines is his for a day. The Mercedes that changed the fate of his family forever. He thinks of his father with a dull ache before driving himself to the next task.

Pappan didn't know Sandhya until Muthalali showed him her picture two days ago. He told him that she was the girl who had ruined his son's life and snatched him away from them all. It was payback time for her now!

The rest of the story was furnished by his mother who made it a habit to resign everything to fate. Even the death of her husband in a tragic car accident involving the Mercedes that Pappan is driving now.

'That girl left for studies abroad after her affair with Mahesh was thwarted. Everything was considered to be settled for the time being. Muthalali, as the whole town knows, had made his son withdraw from it with threat of various kinds. But does love concede defeat so easily? The boy, refusing to forget her, jumped off from the terrace one day.' Pappan's mother narrated the love story dispassionately as if it was a movie.

'And?'

'And what? He didn't die. He became a vegetable.

They moved him from home to the hospital where he lay.

Neither dead, nor alive, until one day life left him.'

A sigh emanated from her womb, a sigh that she drew from an old memory. Then she added, as if to vent her own undisclosed woe, 'Karma. It is the result of

Muthalali's karma. For the things he did to others.'

Pappan knew what she meant by 'things he did to others'. The whole town knew. Like many truths that a society swallows hastily and pushes into its deep innards to escape scalding its tongue, this one too, lay buried amidst deep rumblings. Now and then it belched up, rattling the lungs of those who were affected. Sandhya was only part of the first half of the whole story. The other half included Pappan and his mother.

'Where are you taking me?' Sandhya hollers, angrily. She twists in the backseat as Pappan turns the car towards Muthalali's bungalow. 'You were supposed to take me to Mahesh, not to his father's house!'

For no particular reason, Pappan feels sorry for the girl whose only fault, according to him, was falling in love with an upper caste boy who had a heartless father. He is tempted to tell her what had happened to Mahesh after she left him. The fact that he lay oblivious to the good and bad of life, the fact that the death he had hoped to bring him solace following a heartbreak also betrayed him. That his decision left him dangling in an unspecified realm of consciousness before it finally took pity on him. Above all, the fact that Muthalali held her responsible for whatever had befallen his only son, and sought to get even with her. He is tempted to save the girl from an impending catastrophe.

A snap of realisation jolts Pappan the very next moment. Helping her escape will put his own life in jeopardy. Muthalali has no reputation for compassion and can be remarkably ruthless, especially in this instance involving Mahesh and Sandhya. No one knows it better than Pappan and his mother.

'Why are you bringing me here? You were supposed to take me to Mahesh!' Sandhya screams hysterically as Pappan parks the car, opens the door, and drags her into the sprawling hall of Muthalali's bungalow.

He wonders if there is anyone other than Muthalali inside: his diminutive wife who had shrunk to a shadow with time, or the servants, most of who pledged their loyalty to him more out of fear than good will. The silence and darkness in the adjoining rooms confirms that apart from the man waiting in a plush sofa, watching TV, with none of the villainy that he is fabled to have reflecting on his face, there is not a soul in the house.

'Come, come, my dear girl,' he says with a feigned sense of fondness to Sandhya.

He notices the fearful streaks of tears flushing the bridal make-up down her cheeks and asks Pappan. 'What did you do to her that she is crying? I had asked you to be soft on her. She is, after all, my son's girl.'

'Did he misbehave with you?' he turns to her and asks, in a voice almost mellow. 'What did he tell you? That he will take you to Mahesh?'

Sandhya nods her head, unable to decipher Muthalali's demeanour.

'Which is true, of course. I will send you to Mahesh, because you are rightfully his girl. How can I let you be another man's wife? I made a mistake once. Not again. This time you will unite with him. There is nothing more precious to me than him.'

Pappan feels a chill creep up his feet as Muthalali utters those words with a deliberate stress. He stands tentatively, waiting to be dismissed by Muthalali. Unable to inhale the ominous air that hung heavily in the room, he asks, 'Can I leave, Muthalali?'

Muthalali looks briefly contemplative, and nodding his head gently, as if conceding to Pappan's wish reluctantly, says, 'All right, go. I will take her to Mahesh myself. Being his father, it is actually my duty to unite them. You go on, go.'

Pappan doesn't miss the sinister tone as Muthalali dismisses him with a desultory flick. He heads out of the bungalow, scurrying like a mouse that has just escaped from a cat's paws, and as soon as he crosses the gates, makes a call to the police station from his mobile phone. The ring on the phone is interrupted by the boom of a gunshot not very far behind him. Two more shots follow after a few frozen moments. It takes some effort for Pappan to furnish the policeman at the other end of the line with details.

He sprints across the road, hides behind a soda-beedi shop that has long since closed, and waits for the police jeep to wail into Muthalali's compound. The darkness presses against him and the air is stifling still, but he feels a bizarre sense of relief sweeping over him. The sense of foreboding that held him captive since the early evening begins to wane, and an unusual calm prevails.

In an aching flashback, he thinks of his father and the last conversation they had the night before he died.

No, not died. Killed.

By Muthalali's men at his behest. For aiding Mahesh's affair with Sandhya. For carrying their letters to each other. For ferrying Sandhya from the hostel on the day the couple had planned to elope. For facilitating love.

He remembers his father's words, dripping with dread. 'Muthalali will not spare me for this. If I am killed, take care of your mother.'

A row of rotating strobe lights zip past him and stop in front of Muthalali's massive teak doors. Police jeeps and ambulances. From a distance, he sees two human bodies being moved into the vehicles.

Two.

It all seems surreal again. These wailing moments. The story that brought him here. And its unexpected dénouement.

CHAPTER FOUR

Salma's Silence

For the third week running, there is no internet in the state today. The phones have been lying without use, as if they have lost their sense of purpose. It has been a while since the TV screens in our home flickered too. It feels like we are all in a tunnel—blindfolded and herded by some unknown force to some anonymous destination. We walk for a while, stumbling over things our feet randomly meet and we pause now and then, put our hands out to feel the air around us. There is no palpable sensation on the tip of our fingers. They are frozen perhaps. Or dead. We can't say. If life is determined by breath alone, then we are alive. At least now.

Abbu hasn't come home for two days. We had expected him to return when the curfew was briefly lifted yesterday but it must have been hard to escape his 'call of duty' and his commitment towards our people. That is how he proudly describes his vocation as a journalist. Ammi isn't overly worried about Abbu's absence. She thinks he will be home, sooner or later. I know that she isn't even looking forward to his return. She goes about her work at home, as if nothing has happened—outside our home or inside it.

Winter, officially, is still a few weeks away, but every year, we stock wood early enough. You never know when the restrictions will kick in and when our essential needs will be deemed dispensable by those who have kept us restrained in our little shelters that we call dubiously home. We have got used to living on the edge, as if the only option we have next is to jump into the gorge and disappear with its mist.

'Should we ask Azim Chacha if he saw Abbu anywhere in the last two days?' I ask Ammi, as I help her stack the firewood. Azim Chacha is our neighbour.

'No need.... I have a feeling we should leave them to dry some more. There is a little dampness left in it,' she says inspecting the logs.

Ammi looks older than she should naturally be. There are bags under her eyes that suggest prolonged nights of sleeplessness. They look like reservoirs that hold unshed tears. The blue veins in her hands show up as if they were loath to stay under the skin, impatient to find their own release outside.

She is only a suggestion of the beauty she was before the valley got swathed in the colour of army fatigue. A green different from that of the ageless conifers. Her pale-yellow hijab that once had embroidered motifs on them accentuates the fatigue and bitterness on her face and she looks ready to grab and bite the bullet. If it were to whiz past her anytime, that is.

'You don't have to think so hard about him,' she then says, sharply. 'He will come when he wants to. He knows his way home.'

I am standing so close to her that her words pierce through my ears. They aren't just loud. They are spiteful and severe.

Just then a few logs from the stack roll off and fall next to where we are standing. As I bend to pick them, I notice a wound above her right ankle that she has dressed with a piece of cloth ripped from an old dupatta.

'Ammi, what is this?' I ask, furrowing my brows and dropping the log to examine her leg.

It is not a recent cut. The bandage has soiled and blood has stained over the turmeric powder she had patted on it. It is hard to say if it was still raw beneath. Some wounds are like that. You can never tell if they are healed. Or if they ever will.

'The axe missed the wood last week,' she says casually with a flick of her hand. It was only then that I notice her fore arm under the shawl. There is another bruise that was awaiting oblivion. There is a patch of scalded skin that has begun to reveal the flesh beneath, surrounded by a few purple islands. I wince at the sight. 'Ammi, what is this?' I ask again, my voice expressing apparent alarm.

'Nothing...nothing. These things happen when you are running a home and have a family to look after. You burn your skin when you cook, you hurt your hands and feet when you chop wood, you just get used to it. It is part of a woman's life. You will soon know.'

Ammi forces a smile. It's a sign of resignation to the bleakness that has become her life's truth. Pulling her shawl over the blisters quickly, she instructs me to shut the window. The wind has started getting cold, although the trees are still in the fall phase. The winter could set in early this time.

Outside, the ground wears a carpet of red and yellow leaves. The trees in the vicinity paint a pretty picture, and I let my eyes linger on them before shutting the window. The fall colours are not new to me, but every time I look at them intently, I feel they are saying something to me in an alien language.

Ammi goes to the neighbour's house to ask if there is any change in the hours of the curfew and when it will be lifted. I walk around the room aimlessly, wondering when our life will change for the better. When I would start going to school.

Abbu's absence makes life even more miserable. There is an uncertainty that lurks in the house in his absence. I know that he is out on a mission to make life better for us. He knows a lot more than ordinary people do about the situation out there. He knows the inside stories, the grim reality as it secretly unfolds in the lives of thousands of people like us.

He is a man of great certitude. He has been the voice of our people for as long as I can remember. But it is not easy to be a journalist now. I am worried for him.

Somewhere in the distance I hear the sound of police patrols in whining jeeps. I wonder if there is chaos on the streets now. People protesting, the security men firing and a crowd running helter-skelter, not to save themselves from death, but from being injured and be maimed for life. Death is commonplace for our people. Life is what makes them miserable because no one wants to live without an eye or a limb. It reduces our lives to absolute wretchedness.

I have very little information on what is happening on the streets outside our area. I have not been allowed to step out ever since the lock down fell in place. This autumn has been very restrictive and the farthest that I have ventured is to Azim Chacha's house. His wife is Ammi's close friend and they spend a lot of time together when they have no chores to finish.

Abbu's absence from home gives Ammi the opportunity to live life in her own way. I can notice that she enjoys this freedom—to live outside the glare of her husband. And in turn, I enjoy the freedom of being on my own at home while she is away.

My twin brothers, Salim and Bilawal, are asleep, as they are for most part of the day, happy to be away from school indefinitely. They don't fret as much as me about not meeting friends or not being able to learn. They have no immediate plans for life, except to while it away.

In the silence of our house, I wander a bit, trying to find a way to beat my boredom. Boredom brings sinister thoughts with it, thronging like night insects around a burning wicker. I push the windows open to let the thoughts fly away. But the eeriness in the compound outside depresses me further. I watch the leaves rustle as the wind blows through the fall colour. I listen to its flutter and realise that they were saying something to me. I pay heed, trying hard to make sense.

'Shut the window, and go inside,' they say.

I am frustrated that the golden red leaves have nothing more to tell me than what I have been told time and again.

'Go inside,' Abbu would say every time I went and stood in front of people who came to meet him.

'Why am I always asked to go inside? Why can't I stand there listening to them? I want to know what Abbu is doing in his job. I want to know why people respect him so much,' I said to Ammi once, making my protestation so loud and clear that Abbu had to come in to glower me down into silence.

'You are becoming very impudent these days, Ruhaani,' was his curt reply. And turning to Ammi he said, 'I don't want the two of you lurking here. Take her away. Do I have to teach you how to keep her in leash? Or will you know it yourself?' He hissed through his tobacco-stained teeth.

His stinging words left a frown on my face that refused to leave for days together. It also made me suspect that there was some mystery surrounding Abbu's work. Something that he did not want us to know.

Until then, I had not noticed how Abbu's friends often came to meet him on the stealth after day light. There was something brewing in their midst and it gave me shivers to think of what it could be. Despite his warning to not lurk around, one day I stuck my ear to the door of the room where hc was in a meeting with his friends. I peered through the gap in the door and saw them poring over sheaves of paper. They read out portions from selected ones.

When Abbu's turn came, he turned grim and said, 'I have authentic proof to this. It wasn't a suicide. The girl didn't kill herself. Those bastards left her for dead after ripping her apart. Here is the evidence. I want this to be sent to all national newspapers and media centres anonymously.'

He then passed some papers around. There were some pictures too that the men looked at intently and shook their head in complete disbelief and disapproval. 'Miyan, this is fantastic job. You have nailed them. But you will have to hold it till the situation improves. We cannot make this public yet. We cannot risk your life.'

Abbu seemed to disagree. There was anger in his face. Even through the slender breach I could see that his eyes were turning into fireballs. 'Do you realise that the girl was just 12? The age of my daughter? And you expect me to keep silence over something that I have such clinching evidence about?'

The man sitting next to Abbu put a placating hand on his shoulder and said, 'Patience, miyan. Patience. We share your distress. But we need to keep silence now. Any wrong move from our side could land us in jail, only to rot there till death without even a trial. Let us gather as much evidence as possible against these bastards. Make it fool proof, and then announce it to the people.'

I wondered who they were accusing. Who were they fighting so hard? Who were they trying to nail?

There are times when I wish I was grown enough to know the intrigues that life was throwing around me, in bits and pieces. In silences and shouts.

As the men prepared to disperse, I ran into my room and hid behind the door, guilty of eavesdropping. I stood there waiting for them to leave, thinking at the same time about Abbu and about Salma, my classmate who was found hanging a month ago from a tree behind the mosque. They said it was a suicide. But now Abbu swears it wasn't.

Suddenly, Abbu became a hero to me despite his 'go inside' and his frequent rants to my mother about this and that. He might be an angry man, but not unscrupulous. I promised to Salma that he would bring the bad men who wronged her to justice. Soon. As soon as this lock down was lifted.

But somehow, even after several months now, the lock down continues to sag down the valley like dense mist, refusing to dissipate. And Salma's story remains gagged somewhere inside Abbu's file, waiting to find a voice.

Feeling lonely and clueless, I climb up to my room, my deliberate footsteps on the wooden stair echoing across the silent house, and I snuggle under the woollen rug. Somewhere in the middle of my miscellaneous thoughts about how soon Salma will be released from the theory of suicide, I fall asleep. Another gloomy dusk in the valley pales into a night of uneasy calm.

I coarse into a state of partial dream and partial wakefulness. It's frustrating to wallow in a state like that. The eyes are urging to be opened, but something prevents the eyelids from tearing apart. What makes me aware of this fluid condition, I have not understood. It has happened once before and I asked Ammi about it.

'God,' she said. 'He shines upon us in sleep and lets us into the secrets of the heart.'

What she said wasn't clear to me, but I smiled, because it sounded beautiful.

Somewhere at the far end of this Godly presence in sleep, I hear an unusual commotion. Someone's bawling. It's a woman's voice. My eyes are refusing to open even as the hollering gets louder. I imagine it is Salma. She must be crying out from the pages of Abbu's secret files. I see her brown eyes deepening and becoming gooey. They flow down in a torrent of dirty red.

And then I hear a man's voice thundering over the womanly cry. It is so loud and fierce that I am rattled out of my sleep. My mouth is dry, my hands are sweaty and my heart is pounding inside the rug. Soon it becomes clear to me that the ruckus is real. It is coming from downstairs and not from a dream. It is Abbu's and Ammi's voices.

I wrap the woollen rug around me in fright, unable to stir out of my bed. I wonder if my brothers sleeping in the room next to mine can hear what I am hearing. I feel a numbness come over me as Ammi's voice begins to get shrill. And then, I begin to shiver. Moments of dread pass as the commotion tapers and Ammi's voice dies down. I gather some courage to go down and put my foot down gingerly.

Halfway down, I hear Ammi's voice again. This time it is stern and firm, as if sending out a warning. I can't believe how different it is from her usual plaintive tone.

'No, you won't,' she howls. 'Not anymore.'

'When did you learn to say no to me, you wretch?

Who taught you to defy me? And do you think you can escape me? I am your destiny. Your God. And to serve me selflessly is your creed. Let me see how you can stop me after all these years.'

Abbu's overbearing words sound as if he was daring her. I wonder what he was trying to do to Ammi.

Kill?

What I hear next from Ammi makes my blood run cold.

'Stay away from me. One step more and I will hack you down. I swear upon God.'

I hear the sound of things crashing down and Abbu's shriek shatters the night air. Suddenly, the door to their room creaks open. I crouch in the shadows. What I see in the light streaming out of their room fills me with terror. Ammi is lurching out with a hatchet in her hand. There is blood smeared on its blade and her face. Her hair is a mess and her limbs are unsteady. She sways a little and begins to fall outside the threshold.

'Ammi!' I put my palms to my mouth and give out a loud cry.

She looks up startled and waves her hand urgently.

'Go inside, Ruhaani. Go inside,' she whimpers. Her voice is stretched with pain and seems to pull out from deep within her womb.

I wonder what has happened to Abbu. Has she killed him?

I run across to her in fright but stop when I see Abbu staggering toward the door. Seeing him fills me with dread and my flesh creeps. I struggle to breathe.

'Go Ruhaani,' she cries and heaving with all her might strikes Abbu in the foot.

I don't wait to see what happens to him. I dart to the main door and yanking it open, flee into the narrow alley that leads me to the main street. Army men dot the lanes, their vigilance imparting an unnatural quietness to the unearthly hour.

I feel flakes of the season's first snow falling on me. By morning, the autumn colours will sag under its weight. This place will be shrouded in white. Like Salma's lifeless body and her silence trapped somewhere in Abbu's secret files.

My limbs begin to fail me as I realise that I have no escape. Running into the light can be dangerous. I don't trust the men who are patrolling the place. I have been taught not to. I freeze in my tracks, trembling in the cold wind.

Fear converts to a choking silence in my throat as my eyes blur and become heavy. I sink, put my hand out hoping to find a miraculous hand to save me. Finding none, I kneel, prostrate, and say an ayat.

The rug falls off my shoulder.

No one now tells me, 'Go inside.'

CHAPTER FIVE

BEING ME

It was an announcement no one had expected to come from a seventeen-year-old who was riding high on the wave of an uncommon achievement.

Topper.

100 percent marks.

Then the startling statement was issued. It was as if a bomb had been dropped amidst a carnival.

'Pure Science. That will be her choice,' Dad had said to his colleagues the day the exam results were declared, and they had all nodded in unmistakable admiration for me. The choice was barely a surprise to come from someone who had a perfect score in the subjects that their children struggled to pass muster.

The men in dapper suits and Clarks shoes acknowledged that his daughter was par excellence, and she was all set to be propelled to the next level of academics from where she would go on to create an irreversible success story. They agreed as they congratulated Dad that I had everything on my side to become the next Einstein. Hell, I was all set to bring home a Nobel Prize in due course. A gold medal all the way from Norway was predicted to sit pretty among aplethora of other decorations that I had brought home in my seventeen years of life. It was something Dad had always spoken to them about, and by now, everyone who knew him knew about his grand aspirations for me too.

Mom, for her part, said to her friends that she would love to see me wear the Doctor's coat, cure ailing humans, and save lives. (She always said it in that order.) 'What a noble thing it would be to do! To fix broken hearts!' she exclaimed poetically, seeking approval from her peers.

'Of course, of course,' they said in unison, their festering grudge safely tucked under their heaving bosoms. Some even felt a twinge of jealousy, and rolled their eyes when mom wasn't looking. Mom was certain that a few among them had already started planning the alliance of their son with me and she laughed about it over dinner with Dad and me.

There was no doubt in their minds, that I would bring them the greatest of glories a child was capable of bringing her parents. A glory of the kind that was not envisaged by common people.

With me topping the school board exams, Dad's 'Nobel' dream had inched one step closer home, and he made no attempt to plug his pride.

Mom, being a tad less ambitious, lodged no such towering ideas in her head. She was content with me becoming the best-known heart surgeon in the country. Who decided such things—the best and the rest—I had no clue, but she had always been obsessed with 'excellence', especially in matters pertaining to me.

I had been undaunted throughout, fulfilling their desires, gathering accolade after accolade in everything from academics to music to art, year after year. It was as if

I were pulling out the rabbit of their choice from my hat, as and when they pleased, with no question asked. With no dissent nor digression. Granting their every wish.

Come to think of it, I was in a tearing hurry to complete my obligations towards them and then break free, to lead an unfettered life on my own terms. I knew that day would arrive at some point when I would unfold the wings I had kept tucked under my arms, and fly away to the skies. That it would come this soon was a surprise to me too. It was a spot decision.

The day the results were announced, we had newsmen swooping on us, with dozens of cameras jostling for space and some soundbites from Dad, Mom, and people around. It was curious to see them all making celebrities out of us when all I had done was bring home a perfect score in my board exams.

Somewhere down the years, numbers and grades had stopped being a fetish to me. This excess fuss over an accomplishment was insufferable to me.

I watched the beavering pack of newsmen with wonder and felt seriously tickled by their questions.

'How does it feel to be the most intelligent teenager in the country?'

Most intelligent? Really?

'Unbelievable,' was all I said, because that was what I had heard my predecessors say.

To a few others who shoved the mic in front of me, I said, 'It feels good,' faking a squeal.

In reality, I wanted to confess to them that it all felt a little bizarre to be tagged 'the most intelligent' when that claim could not be ratified. How could they say I was the best student in the country based on a standardised test of a few hours? I could probably be described as an ace crammer, a rote specialist or something equally wacky, but certainly not the most intelligent in the whole country.

Dad and Mom gushed with pride as packets of sweets began to get stacked on the side table. They waited for their turn with the reporters. I had even caught Mom rehearsing her lines in front of the mirror an hour before. The neighbours who had gathered to congratulate us looked on with awe, eager to grab their sixty seconds of fame in the frame, and the newsmen competed with each other to ask the most ridiculous questions to me.

'Did your parents sit with you while you burnt the midnight oil?'

No, they were busy making love at that time. 'Did you think you'd top the whole country?' Of course. The astrologer had predicted it.

'What advice will you give your juniors who have their eyes set on this spot in the coming years?'

God save you from the dreams of other people.

'Is this something you have been planning from a young age?'

Not a young age. From the day I was conceived. I have been planning this from my days as an embryo.

There were moments when I wished that it were all a bad dream. I didn't want any of it, least of all the drama that was unfolding in front of me.

For a blurry moment, I imagined myself telling them, 'Oh, you are all so mistaken. It isn't even me. I didn't even take the exams. There was this apparition that appeared in front of me a few minutes before the exam, all wired up and weird looking. I pushed it into the exam hall while I went gallivanting in the town with my boyfriend. That day, he kissed me for the first time in places I cannot tell you. It is a secret, don't let my parents know about it.' I giggled inwardly at that point, imagining the consternation in the faces before me.

It wasn't me at all who gave the exams and got this damn thing...this...whatever you are celebrating, I protested, silently. It was a robot that was crafted out of me. An inanimate object that supplicates to your commands. Why, I have even forgotten my name! I am now only a dream-fulfilling machine for my parents and an envy generating idol for my friends. For the rest, like you all, it doesn't even matter what I am.

The press meet went on amidst these thoughts roiling inside me. The heart waited impatiently to release the resentment I had kept bottled up for years. Flanked by Dad and Mom, I rehearsed my lines in the head. It didn't matter what the question was, the answer was fixed.

I was asked to speak of my feelings of gratitude, next steps, etc. before the specific questions were to be fired at me again.

This was it.

'Thank you,' I began, softly, running a nervous glance across the room. 'Thank you, everyone, for your generous words of praise and appreciation. Thank you, Dad and Mom, for making me what I am today. Before I am asked how I feel and what I plan for my future, let me tell you all a thing. Dad, Mom, I am sorry if I disappoint you. You are not used to being disappointed by me. Hence when you hear this, it might hurt you several times more than it might parents of average students as you term them.'

I saw their faces stiffen as I spoke those words. My mouth felt dry, and I swallowed hard. The audience fell into an uneasy silence, the feverish moments ticking as I paused to gather courage.

'I don't intend to study further. This is the end of my academics. I have no plans for my future....'

Just as a reporter began to ask a question, Dad raised his hand to stop him and rose to his feet.

I shut my eyes tight as I felt his grip on my arm. Surprisingly, there was no animosity in his touch. I had expected him to drag me inside, but all he did was to make me sit in the chair and asked Mom to fetch some water.

Mom hobbled in with panic. The audience seized the opportunity and began to fling questions at us.

'I don't think she will be in a position to take your questions. I request you all to kindly disperse and respect our privacy,' Dad announced. It sounded like what families of celebrities said to the media when they died mysteriously.

What an irony that it had come close to it, but the tragedy was averted only because of my firm decision to quit.

The buzz in the room lasted for half an hour, after which the house plunged into a quietness that reminded me of the days preceding the exams.

I didn't know what to expect from Dad and Mom, but this scene had been recreated in my mind several times, with changing effects. Except, I hadn't told them the entire thing yet. They hadn't heard me out in full and the uncertainty that lingered gave the evening a ghostly aspect. As if it was all a dystopian dream.

I wondered in what realm of consciousness I was floating at that time. What do you call that space where you are neither happy nor sad, waltzing in a desensitised land? Stoicism? No, the word sounded too lofty for comfort to my ears. I let it be. It didn't matter. Not anymore.

Dad and Mom were engaged in a serious conversation inside their room. I made no attempt to eavesdrop, nor did I agonise over what they might be discussing. They would soon present themselves in front of me, to cross-examine me, and to demand an explanation. I steeled myself up to face their wrath or whatever it was that they would spew on me. Mom's sullen tears. Dad's morbid stare. Their clouded faces and the shadows they would cast on me. There would be a huge display of emotions for me to contend with. Gross from Mom. Grave from Dad.

Clearly, it wouldn't be easy for them to see their dreams come crashing down like that, in a snap. The ticket to Oslo, the Doctor's coat, the pride of place in society—these wouldn't be easy to renounce. They had spun a life around it, spent all their emotions and energies on it for several years.

I lay prone in the sofa relishing the sweet void that was filling within me as I contemplated my life from here. I imagined the universe with its arms open wide, waiting to sync itself with me.

As the uncertainty of the evening wore on, hunger pangs began to seize me and I zombie-walked into the kitchen and rummaged in the fridge. I opened the containers inside and found leftovers from lunch. As the sharp smell of garlic-laced curries stung my nostrils, I realised my craving was not for food. I didn't want to satiate the stomach, but I felt an intense urge to satisfy a desire that I could not quite put my finger on. Where did it rise from? What would assuage it?

I discovered a family pack of butterscotch ice-cream inside the freezer that had found its way home long before the exams. It had lain there half-consumed, gathering freezer odour, for nearly two months. After all, cold or cough during the exams could have put paid to Dad and Mom's Himalayan hopes for me.

But it was all over now, and I devoured the treat frantically, feeling the cold cut through my tongue and throat. A poor tooth, waiting for its turn at the dentist, moaned faintly as the ice-cream washed over it.

The dull ache in the tooth was instantly supplanted by the pleasure of the palate. I dumped the empty bucket into the trashcan, feeling relief in the nooks and crannies of my whole being. How futile life had been without its share of Baskin Robbins!

I felt alive again, as alive as I had before the seasons of expectations, and ambitions had begun. Before the racetrack was laid out for me to run and win. Before my accolades became an addiction to Dad and Mom. Before my life changed to a lame, naked, hollowed-out semblance of a teen.

'Simmy?'

It was Dad from the living room. His voice was feebler than what it usually was.

I gulped the ice-cream laced saliva, cleared my throat, and hurried out. Inquest time. The distance from the kitchen to the living room seemed like an eternity.

'Dad, two minutes,' I said and rushed to the bathroom. I briefed myself as I sat on the pot for longer than it was required.

I had to remain calm and solemn in front of him. The last thing I wanted him to imagine was that I was joking or that I was out of my mind. I had to convince him that I had made my decision consciously, knowing precisely what it meant.

It meant that I was giving up everything that was hitherto considered important in my life.

It meant hanging up a festooned future that I had come so painfully close to.

It meant standing up and speaking for myself at the impressionable age of 17.

It meant finding and being myself before they could usurp me.

Dad looked tired but determined in the wan light of the ornate corner lamp. Mom was nowhere in sight. She had probably left it to him to complete the task of grilling. It was a sensible decision, I thought, given her propensity for theatrics.

'Dad, I am sorry,' I said, standing in front of him.

Despite my best efforts, I couldn't stop my eyes from filling up. I wasn't sure if I was sorry, but an apology seemed appropriate, for the level of my transgression wasn't small. I had consciously sought to crush his dreams, with the ruthlessness unbecoming of a child. I had become a metaphor for filial ingratitude.

'Hmm...' he grunted. 'Mom wants you to eat and go to sleep.'

'Dad...'

'It's late and I am tired. You must get some sleep too. We can talk tomorrow. There is nothing that cannot wait until then.'

I wished the lights were bright for me to read his face and decipher his thoughts.

I wished he let me vent my heart and gave my freedom right away.

'Dad,' I said again, moving closer to him.

He took my hand, patted it, and said, 'Tomorrow.'

There was no bitterness in his voice.

Even in the dim settings and through the blur in my eyes, I saw that there was no malice in his eyes. I didn't know if I was imagining, but there was a suggestion of a smile in his handsome, half-century young face. For once, I felt genuinely sorry for what I was doing to him. 'Good night, Dad,' I whispered and left the room carrying with me an ambivalence inspired by Dad's unexpectedly mild manner.

The unspoken things between us had to wait for a night before they could be voiced and sorted out, and along with them, my long-awaited freedom to set out on a life of my choice.

I vaguely remember having wept into my pillow that night. I don't remember why.

Thinking of it now, decades later, it seems like an episode from another lifetime. Fuzzy and fogged out.

CHAPTER SIX

That Pain in The Womb

No one believed Badri could do it. Least of all, his mother, Kamla.

He wasn't home when the police came looking for him in his asbestos-roofed shanty in the heart of the city. Crowds lingered on the edges of the alley that led to his house, appalled that one of their own should be an accused in the case that had shaken the country a week ago.

They were not a perfect community. They had frequent street brawls over money and space, rarely over religion, and almost always had a couple of domestic fights going on. They had their fair share of thieves and thugs living amongst them, petty criminals who got by in life with meagre pickings here and there, and even some rumoured hit men serving the city's underworld. This background made the coming and going of policemen a common sight for the people living there.

This, however, was unprecedented. It was the first time that someone in their midst had committed such a heinous crime—rape and murder. And of such monstrous proportions? Badri? Their Badri?

They refused to believe it. Either their estimation about him had been too naïve or the police were making a huge mistake in tagging him with the crime.

'Are you the boy's mother? Where is he?' The man who led the team of not less than ten policemen thundered as they barged into the tight two-room structure with light blue walls.

Two men menacingly stood outside to keep the crowds at bay. As if to show off their bravado, they kicked things they found before them into the gutter that ran along the long stretch of tin houses.

'He hasn't come home for three months, sir. He went saying he has found a job in Delhi,' said Kamla. After a quivering pause, she asked, 'What has he done, sir?'

The man pierced a glance at her. It was filled with equal amounts of wrath, contempt, and an impatience to dispense justice.

'Do you watch news on TV? Your son was among those four heroes,' he said, adding a mocking inflection on the last word.

It took a while for Kamla to catch the drift of what he had just said. And just as it dawned on her, she put her hand to the mouth and wheezed hard. 'He hasn't done anything. You are mistaken. He isn't that kind, sir. I know, my child isn't capable of doing it. I beg, in the name of God, please spare him.'

'Check every nook and cranny,' the Inspector instructed his men, who pulled down everything they could lay their hands on.

'He is a child of sixteen years! You must have got it wrong, sir. Spare him. He isn't capable of doing it. It is a mother's word. She knows it here when her child goes wayward,' Kamla said, briefly touching her stomach, swearing by a mother's gut feeling.

She had also wanted to reiterate that Badri had long since left Mumbai. He had found a job as a cleaner in a big hospital in Delhi. So, whatever they claimed about his involvement, couldn't be true.

The Inspector guffawed, knocking a table-fan off a stool, and ripped the calendar off the wall. 'What did you say? Child? He seems to have accomplished quite a bit as a child then,' he curved his lips and tilted his head to show disdain. 'He is a beast. Do you hear? A beast. And we are going to get him soon.'

There was enough foreboding in the Inspector's voice to make Kamla quake. Her breath wavered as she watched the policemen ransack her house, searching for evidence that she knew didn't exist. She also knew they had arbitrarily concluded that Badri was among the men who have been dominating the news on TV for a week now. Three faces had been revealed on the screen but the identity of the fourth one was kept concealed. He was a juvenile, they said. But how was she to even imagine that the face behind the blotted picture was her son?

Thinking of it now, Kamla realised that the rest of the details about the blurred perpetrator's background matched with her son. They precisely knew that he came from the slum, was a school drop-out, and that his grandparents had migrated from a village in Rajasthan. It just didn't strike upon her, not in the slightest bit, that it would be Badri.

The entire country was in uncontainable rage. The police force was on a rampage and had to, at the earliest, nab the men who thought nothing of tearing into a young woman and in the end, burn her alive with petrol. It all happened in an old, abandoned warehouse in the heart of the city.

'What was he doing here before he ran away from home?'

'He didn't run away. He went for work. To Delhi. Three months ago,' the indignation in her voice was unexpected.

She thought of how she had tried everything in her means to get him to finish school but he insisted on earning money and standing on his own feet. His ambition was to go to the Gulf. He wanted to be a rich man and live in a tall building. He wanted to buy his mother a Benarasi silk saree. He wanted to marry an actress. But he never wanted to rape a woman. Never.

Nobody in the neighbourhood came to offer Kamla solace that night. No one reassured her that it was all a case of mistaken identity, that they all knew her son too well to believe it. No one, except her daughter, Rupa who lived with her family a few clusters away. She came enquiring but she too had very little to say to Kamla and left quickly citing her child's fever. This was a mess no one wanted to get involved with.

Kamla sat in the middle of the raided house, unable to make sense of what had transpired during the day. She had spent the whole evening ranting out to the world from the pit of her stomach that the police were merely finding scapegoats; that the poor had no power in this lopsided world and that injustice was their inherited destiny.

As the routine commotion of a day in the slum subsided, an eerie quietness prevailed outside, except for the cacophony from TV sets. Kamla heard a mélange of loud reporting from TV anchors competing for the country's attention on the case. She wondered what lies and fabricated stories the newsmen were saying about her son.

She slowly gathered herself up from where she lay in a heap since the raid, and reached out to turn the TV on, but no channel showed up. The silent screen complimented the blue walls as Kamla saw that the cables from the TV had been pulled out by the policemen.

She walked towards the door and stared into the bleak, malevolent night, not knowing what the next day would bring. She smelled of sweat, and all the crying in the day had made her eyes sore. She picked a paint canister that was now used as a pail and hobbled down the lane to the public tap. The tap hissed a little before water began to trickle, followed by a feeble flow. She emptied the pail over her head and washed off all her fears.

The night breeze made her shiver, but she stood there, firming up her belief that the boy whose face remained hidden on TV screens was not her son. This anonymity was her greatest solace for now. Only the name was the same and the police will soon discover that they were two different people.

Kamla stepped into the kitchen to find it in complete disarray. The flour and rice tins had been knocked down spilling its content all over, and she found that the money and a gold chain she had kept hidden in the rice tin were missing. The bastards had stolen even that. She tried to salvage whatever little she could from the spilled supplies.

There was no means to talk to her daughter as the police had confiscated her old Nokia cell phone too. Her daughter called her every two days and Badri called once in a while. He did not give her a number to call back, of course. Badri told her that his number kept changing and he would call her whenever he could.

'Is the job very arduous? Are you eating well?' she asked him. It was a given that when you become a migrant worker, you are treated as an outsider. In essence, this meant you had less privileges, meagre salaries, and no voice to raise against any act of injustice by the boss.

He parried her question with a, 'You don't worry about me, Amma. I am very well, busy making a life.'

What he did not tell her was that he wasn't working in a hospital as she was given to understand. At sixteen, he felt like he owned his life and was answerable to no one. Not even his mother.

One day, he made a call from a friend's phone and said, 'I have lost my phone. I may not be calling you till I get a new one...and I cannot say when.'

It was the last time she had spoken to her son.

In the morning, Rupa made another hurried visit, mainly to announce that her in-laws did not approve the idea of her visiting her mother often.

'I have to abide by them. You understand, don't you? But I will call to check on you every two days,' she said, her tone revealing more of her helplessness than any attempt to comfort.

'It is not necessary. My phone is with the police,' said Kamla coldly from the cot, where she had been lying since the last night in her wet clothes. She had no strength in her bones to wake up and go to work. She had no will to step out of the room and face the world that by now would have stamped her as a rapist's mother.

Her feeble voice and droopy disposition made her daughter worry, but there was very little she could do. She belonged in another place, had another life that she could not put on the line. 'Please understand, Amma.'

'It's all right. It's all right,' she waved.

'I am going to get something for you to eat.'

'Tell me honestly, do you think our Badri would do such a thing?'

Rupa looked at her pitifully and walked out. She really didn't know the answer.

Rupa discreetly avoided locking eyes with people who crossed her way. She covered her head with the dupatta, more to conceal her face than to evade the late morning sun. There was nothing she could do for her mother, not even give her the false hope of Badri not being the accused juvenile on the run. After all, he wasn't on the run anymore. The police had apprehended him in a train going to Kolkata and the breaking news said that he had confessed to the crime.

She knew at one glance that the boy the policemen pushed and shoved in and out of the jeep was her brother, despite the cloth that covered his face.

As she dodged the noisy children scampering in the narrow lane she wondered if she must disclose the morning news to her mother. She felt her mother had a right to know. Especially with the TV in the house not working, she might remain ignorant of the reality until someone broke it to her.

Inside the house, Kamla tried to sit up. She did not have any particular objective but she has been laying there for so long that she hoped things must have changed for the better in the interim.

She had to have an answer from Rupa without fail when she returned, she thought. Did she think Badri was capable of doing such a heinous crime?

'It doesn't matter what I think, Amma. He has been caught.

And the morning news update says he has confessed to being a part of the whole thing,' Rupa said impassively while passing a samosa to her mother.

The plate dropped from Kamla's hand, spilling its contents on the floor.

Rupa sat next to her mother and said, slowly but firmly. 'Amma, you are to blame for it. You never spanked him when he erred, right from childhood. You always found a reason to yell at me, for small things like not chopping the onion in thin slices or wearing my dupatta the right way. You treated us differently!'

Kamla began to protest with a deep moan and a frantic wave of her hand, but Rupa continued.

'He was your favourite, deserving of your indulgent love and forgiveness. And I was always someone destined to be another man's and family's property, and so grooming me to fit their settings was more important to you than loving. You couldn't let me be imperfect because I was a girl. Yet you never questioned him when he came home late or suspected him when the money in your rice tin went missing. He could do all that he pleased. Especially, after father died.'

Kamla looked at her with consternation. 'You believe the lies those bastards are saying, but will not trust a mother's instincts? What if someone speaks similar things about your son after he grows up? Will you buy it?' she thundered.

'If the law proves he has done it, then I will not defend him. I will not let my maternal love cloud my sense of right and wrong.'

She continued after a pause, 'A month ago, I caught my eight-year-old stealing money from his father's purse. It was to buy chocolates from a shop near his school, he said. I called it stealing, while my mother-in- law called it a childish prank,' she shook her head at the thought of it. 'I didn't relent, I didn't want to follow you.'

As she was speaking, her phone rang. It was her husband.

'I must go now, Amma. I will try to send someone to fix your TV.'

Before she crossed the threshold, she felt it necessary to tell her mother that Badri indeed was the accused juvenile. 'There is no use denying it. He has confessed and narrated every little detail of that night.'

As the horror of what Rupa had just said sank in, panic gripped her. Kamla wailed and struck her head a few times with her palm. She shuddered to think of what her son must have undergone at the hands of the police, but said nothing, not because she knew Rupa would have none of it, but because Kamla's conviction itself was now waning. It was hard for her to determine what was true and what was not.

She gulped two glasses of water to douse the rising disquiet, squeezed her eyes shut, put her hand to her stomach and whispered, 'What a wicked womb this is!'

Two weeks later, after the three men and the juvenile were proven guilty beyond doubt in a fast-track court, Rupa visited her mother to find her in a state of complete decrepitude. It seemed like she hadn't bathed or eaten in days. No one in the neighbourhood had even checked on her. She wondered if people deserted each other out of fear or apathy. Either way, in times of abject despair, everybody is essentially alone, she concluded.

For her own part, the day the court pronounced her brother guilty, she had tried to sneak out to meet her mother but her attempts were foiled by a stern warning from her husband. She said nothing, did not even make an appeal to allow her to meet her lonely mother who must be wallowing in her misery all alone.

She was afraid of what—of ruining her marital life, of looking her mother in her sorrow-laden eyes, of the diabolical shadow her brother's conviction would cast on her children? Or was it all of it? She did not know.

On the other hand, she felt guilty of not being around her mother when she might have needed her the most, but in her defence, life often forced one to be selfish for the sake of one's own well-being. It made one avoid the truth for the fear of being consumed by it. It might be a coward's way, but she decided she would not visit her mother for at least two weeks. She did what Kamla's neighbours had done to her.

She, however, sneaked out a day after the verdict came, risking everything she was afraid of losing.

The house was not locked from inside and she pushed it open nervously. She found her mother lying curled up in the cot, occupying a corner as if she had shrivelled to half her size in two weeks.

'Amma,' Rupa gently tapped her.

She was in the same clothes that she was the last time Rupa had met her. She was in a state of delirium, weakened by days of starving and neglect.

Rupa shook her harder, this time with a racing heart. She put her fingers in front of her mother's nostrils. She was breathing. Rupa sighed.

'Amma, wake up,' she said, raising her voice further, and sprinkled water on her face.

Kamla opened her eyes a crack, barely acknowledging Rupa's presence.

'What have you made of yourself, Amma?'

Kamla stirred a bit and grunted feebly. Wrapping her dupatta around her waist and tucking it in, Rupa went around the cot, propped her mother's frail body up and rested her against the blue wall that was beginning to peel off in places.

Rupa made her sip some water and opened the tiffin that she had smuggled from her house. Kamla showed no interest in the food and kept pushing it away until Rupa lost her patience.

'What do you want do? Starve and die? All right, do it. Do it for a son who spared no thought for you before he did those terrible things. Do it because you think it will undo everything that is happening. Do it so that I can spend the rest of my life in grief and guilt.'

Until now, Rupa had been pretending not to be affected by the recent events for the sake of her family. She had always maintained a distance between her two families, but it was getting increasingly difficult for her to remain untouched. Finally, she surrendered to her suppressed sentiments. She gulped a glass of water before slumping on the floor. She imagined her brother in police custody being steamrolled to confess as her mother chose to believe. She then thought if he was genuinely capable of doing whatever he was convicted for.

He was the son her parents had yearned to have after two daughters, the younger one of whom died in infancy. They had waited long for him to be born. Her mother had lived in the fear of being abandoned by her husband should she not bear him a son. She took sacred vows of the extreme nature and fulfilled them for a son to be placed in her womb. Once after a miscarriage, she had even tried to take her own life by swallowing a wild, poisonous fruit.

What had saved her then, only providence knows, but she survived to finally give birth to a son twelve years after Rupa was born. It was unimaginable that the son had earned shame so early in life. It was as if he bore a wicked seed in his heart from birth, which sprouted and spread even before he became an adult. How soon the blue-eyed boy of his parents had fallen!

To Rupa, it was justice in some ways. Secretly, she felt that the despise she had harboured for Badri in the

years after he was born was vindicated now.

He had got more of everything from her parents— love, forgiveness, food, and every other indulgence that they could afford. Rupa had reconciled to his pampered existence only for one reason. Her parents allowed her to go to school and paid her fee. Then her father died in an accident at his work site and everything changed.

'Amma, eat something. I will give you a sponge bath and leave. I can't stay long,' she said, wearily.

'Where is he now? In jail?' Kamla asked, her voice barely audible.

'In a shelter home. That's where they put convicts under eighteen. Not in a jail.'

Kamla moaned as if to express relief that her son was not in a jail. 'Shelter Home' sounded more like a safe place.

She was convinced that there was no fairness in the judgment. Her son was accused and convicted for something that she knew he could not have committed. She had no doubt in her mind about his innocence and she repeatedly said that he had been framed by some evil-minded people around him. She wondered why the charm she had got from the temple, imbued with prayers, blessings, and good luck didn't protect him from the evil influences.

'Amma, if you start eating and get better soon, I will take you to meet him at the shelter home,' said Rupa as she dipped a towel into the lukewarm water and rubbed Kamla's arms patiently.

'Will he be in handcuffs? It will break my heart to see him in that state. My poor child. But do take me to him. I want to hear from him just once that he hasn't done anything. That he has been wrongly held guilty.'

'And then do what? Fight for him in the court? Can you challenge the verdict with only your maternal love for proof of his innocence?'

'I just want to hear from him,' Kamla repeated.

All she wanted was to exonerate her son in her heart. She could not bear the thought of anything contrary.

Living with the burden of having given birth to a wicked child was akin to self-torture. And she did not want to spend another day bearing that unspeakable burden.

'Let's go tomorrow,' she said, eagerly.

'Next month. Chotu's papa and his mother are going to Benaras for three days for his father's annual ritual,' she said, looking into the fallow eyes of Kamla and searching for some trace of life in them.

The odd feeling of pity for her mother returned and Rupa was surprised that her heart felt no pain for what had happened to her brother.

Why did they give Badri a bigger portion of their love than her? She never asked because she knew the answer. In their skewed version of the world, boys always got a little extra of everything. It was a distortion that she was determined to correct by treating her son and daughter equally.

Her husband's concurrence with it, despite her mother-in-law's outdated views, made her a proud wife. He was a serious man, but not as uncharitable as many other men were. If she appealed to him politely, he might even let her visit her mother every day till she recovered.

It took two weeks for Kamla to get to her feet and amble about the house. She had lain there, with nothing to feed her delirious mind except the recurring thought that it was all untrue. She had no one to seek an endorsement of her belief. Rupa chose not to comment on it.

'Amma, we are going tomorrow to see him,' she said when she came to visit three Sundays later.

'Can we carry something for him? I don't know what they must be feeding him. My poor child.'

Rupa nodded grudgingly. It still irked her that her mother had such soft corner for her convict son. Daughters could never beat sons in the race for their mother's love.

'I will cook for him. Will they let me feed him?'

'How will I know?' Rupa snapped. 'Have I been there before?'

'Get me some provisions and vegetables from the store before you go home, will you? Let me prepare a feast.'

This was ridiculous. In all these years that she had been married, not once had her mother prepared a feast for her and her family. Here she was, all geared up to cook a treat for her rapist son. How deplorable could it get!

Rupa suppressed a sniffle behind her dupatta and turned away.

For the first time in several weeks, the aroma of fried fish and onions wafted out of Kamla's house. She was up early, pumping the stove and putting the menu in place. Rice, lentils, fish fry, and roasted potatoes were packed in quantities that could last Badri a few days.

'Do you expect him to eat a week's worth of food today itself?' Rupa mocked her mother as she tasted each of what was cooked. She was faintly pleased that her mother had left a portion for her to have before they left. Kamla chose to ignore the disdain in her daughter's tone. She had accepted Rupa's despise for Badri as irrevocable, no matter how hard she tried to tell her daughter that she treated them both equally.

Today, she had other things on her mind, and her daughter's caustic remarks failed to evoke any response in her. She made sure that she had packed everything, and before leaving, lit the lamp at the altar.

Rupa waited at the door, unsure of what she felt at the prospect of meeting Badri. He was her sibling but she hated him. Now he was a criminal too. How was she supposed to feel?

On their way to the reformatory, in the auto- rickshaw, Kamla held Rupa's hand, the nervousness palpable as she squeezed it. It was as if she had deposited all her hope of having her son exonerated in that firm grip. Rupa felt a fleeting sense of pity for her mother. For one moment, she hated her brother more than ever before just for shattering their mother's trust. Her love for him was blind and yet how brazenly he had trampled on it with his reprehensible act!

'Are you nervous, Amma?'

Kamla nodded, her eyes glistening with restrained tears. 'What will I tell him, Rupa?'

Rupa had no answer. What indeed did a mother tell her son on such an odd occasion as this!

The man at the gate of the reformatory wanted to know who they were going to see. Rupa had all the necessary papers to show their identity. She avoided looking into the gateman's eyes for the fear of seeing disgust in it. Or will it be pity for her mother, for begetting a son who in the whole nation's eyes didn't deserve to live? But live he will, they all knew, and that would be an added reason for the gatekeeper to hate her. The home was full of young boys of all ages, and it took a while for Rupa to realise that they were all there for a bad reason. Rupa reminded herself to hold Kamla back when Badri walked in to keep her from lunging at him. Watching her mother hugging her rapist son was something she couldn't have tolerated.

When at last he arrived, Kamla stiffened, unable to utter anything and began to cry. Badri had changed a lot since they had seen him last. He had grown into a man from a boy. It was a telling change, something that validated his crime.

He sat next to Kamla and said nothing.He refused to look into her face and replied only in nods and monosyllables to whatever Kamla asked.

'Do you get good food here?'

He nodded.

Kamla waited for him to look up, so she could gaze into his eyes and see the truth in it but he was stoic. There was no shade of sentiment in his face.

In the end, Kamla spoke, her tension reaching a breaking point. 'I don't want to believe anything that they say. Just once, let me hear it from you that none of this is true.'

'I am hungry. Have you brought me food?' he asked.

Kamla hurried to open the tiffin carrier and asked the guard if she could feed him.

'You have five minutes,' he said.

As she scooped some rice with her fingers, Rupa noticed her hands shiver. She felt a lump in her throat as tears welled up in Badri's eyes and began to course down. Kamla, unmindful of it, fed him a few mouthfuls.

'Amma...' he began to speak.

'No, don't speak while eating. The food will get into your wind-pipe and choke you.'

Rupa watched her brother as he struggled to swallow the rice. He refused to eat the fish saying it made him nauseous.

After a few rounds of feeding, Kamla stopped, and looking into Badri's eyes said, 'Will you forgive this mother for what she is doing? It is God's wish that the womb that gave birth to a life chooses to take that life. Not because I believe what people say, but because I cannot let the two of us live with this blot for a whole lifetime.'

Rupa's face turned white as she gathered the import of her mother's words. Before she could react, Kamla helped herself to a few mouthfuls of rice and lentils. She had never seen her mother eat so greedily.

There was a murderous intent in her face that was neither rage nor regret. Just a sense of having dispensed justice for a grave mistake she had committed—that of mothering a son whom she could neither pardon nor hold guilty. She couldn't have punished him without punishing her womb for allowing the evil in him to sprout, grow, and manifest as a child.

The pain she felt in the space that conceived him couldn't have found any other way to subside.

CHAPTER SEVEN

THE RIVER CHILD

'You were born to me and a river!'

Mamma would say this to me every time I asked her about my father. And then she would slip into a story-weaving mode all over again. She made my birth sound like a fairy tale that I listened to wide-eyed, but never with doubt. It was my truth through childhood, one that wasn't challenged until time came of age and introduced rational ideas into my maturing mind.

Many times, the story became a lullaby as Mamma sang slowly,

I conceived you at the foothills of a mountain kingdom. It was a season of rain.

With green slopes as far as eyes could see during the day, And at night, the moon shimmering all over.

I conceived you by the moon-river With stars standing witness to it.

'What does conceive mean?' I asked her one day.

'Conceive means...,' she paused at that point, bit the corner of her lip, and then slowly whispered, 'Create.'

The way she uttered the word 'create' made me imagine that she and a river had sat together under a flowering tree and had sculpted me out of soft, brown clay lovingly—baby part by baby part coming alive. It made me feel I was very special, unlike any other child in the neighbourhood who were all born of human beings. No one had a river for a father, I gloated inwardly, and then I asked mother the closing question, 'When will I see him?'

A faint smile dotted her angelic face, she planted a kiss on my forehead before tucking me into bed, and said, 'When you grow up.'

Growing up took a long time, and somewhere along the way, the story of my birth shed its sheen. Years of listening to the same story had caused boredom to set in and at some point, mother too stopped talking to me about it.

Even the best of fantasies can get blunted if one dwells upon it for too long.

It was in my fourteenth year that the myth was finally shattered. When I wrote in a school composition that my father was a river, there was no conviction in the statement that for so long had been my truth. In honesty, it was a truth which with time had become a suspicion, and I feared would soon turn out to be a lie. On that day, however, knowing no one else to call as my father, I wrote what I had been told.

The whole class laughed its head off when I read it aloud. The teacher quietened them and said to me gently that rivers don't sire children, and asked me from where I had acquired that piece of fiction.

Later in the afternoon, when I was putting my books in the locker before leaving school, Kevin, the burliest boy in the class came and said, mischief dripping from his face, 'Baby, you need some lessons in making children,' and took me with him. That day, I learnt some new truths that made the moon-river the biggest lie in my life.

'Your river story is a goddamn lie, isn't it?' I bawled as soon as I reached home.

Mamma was unperturbed. She was more concerned about the fact that I hadn't shown up from school at the usual hour.

Her reticence made me suspicious. It was as if she had waited for this revelation to happen sooner or later. There was no alarm of having been exposed as she laid the table for dinner, neatly as always, as if we had guests coming in. But that's how she was always—meticulous and unhurried in her ways. Yet, her silence on the subject was disconcerting and I demanded an answer.

'It wasn't a lie,' she said, calmly. She took the candle sticks that came out only on special occasions, and put them at the centre of the table. 'It isn't the truth either,' she further said, lighting three silver spiral candles with such peace radiating from her face that together with the candlelight, it made the room look like a hillside chapel.

With that the conversation ended.

It is crushing to think that it was the last time Mamma and I had sat together for dinner, it was the last time we spoke to each other, and it was the first and the last time I had felt so much animosity for her in my heart.

Who knew that in that brief disclosure of her past lay her end?

Who in the heaven had ordained that the pain that she had carried for fourteen years had to terminate so painfully—in pools of blood soaked up by the pink bed spread that she had recently embroidered?

I often think of the moments that must have preceded her decision to quit. Sometime in the middle of the night, when the demons of her past came and ambushed her in sleep, unable to fight them, she must have drawn the line.

A ruthless gash that seeped her life out in red trickles that became slow streams.

What does it take to convert a moment of absolute despair into a slice of freedom? How did one turn an agonising thought to a violent act of self-destruction? It is beyond me.

It is difficult to say what was more devastating—the thought that I was orphaned or the realisation that mother had taken away the secret of my birth with her. The only piece of truth she had left behind for my immediate discovery was a hurriedly written note that I found under her pillow two days later.

It read, 'How will I tell you the truth, darling, when I don't know it myself?'

That is how 'knowing our truth' became the mission of my life.

The monsoons have made the river swell and surge dramatically. It is in a frenetic mood today. It almost felt like, if offered, it would take my life to the distant seas from where I could take off to the horizons.

Twenty-three years ago, Mamma must have spent her days delighting in this heavy, moist atmosphere. She had come here to take a slice of this serenity and tuck it into her life after she broke up with her long-time boyfriend. Like Elizabeth Gilbert in Eat, Pray, Love.

A year-long stint at the sanatorium back home did very little to fix the fractures in her soul and she took a plane to India, where she had heard even the darkest nights found enlightenment. It was here that she thought her life would find that missing piece of sanity and stability.

'Don't sit by the river so late. There are snakes in the river.' A voice from behind startles me. 'Snakes?'

'Yes, when the current is forceful, they slide up the steps to where you are sitting. You'd better leave.'

It is the security man who watches over the private ghat attached to the ashram where I am staying.

There is only a little light in the ghat, falling from the street slightly up ahead, but it is enough for me to spot a snake should one slither up to me. If I am watchful, that is.

I think of the snakes in the river and of Mamma. Didn't anyone advise her not to stay so close to the river so late in the night?

'How long have you been here?' I ask the man who had his head wrapped in a red and white chequered cloth to protect himself from the mist that floated over the river and its sacred precincts.

He doesn't seem to have a fear of snakes. He doesn't have to. He is a man. Men don't get attacked by snakes. At least, not the way Mamma was.

'Several years.'

'Then you will know!' I exclaim as I spring to my feet and sprint towards where he stood. I had to be careful not to trip on the steps and fall.

'Know what?' he says, indifferently.

'Know what happened that night,' I mumble, indistinctly.

I notice in the wan light that trickled in from the street that the man has a beard, though not entirely black. He must be past his middle-age, I make an estimate. I look urgently into the dim glint in his eyes, as rain begins to fall.

'You must go now. The rain will get harder, and it isn't safe anymore,' he urges and starts walking back.

Didn't he hear what I was demanding to know? Or didn't he want to answer?

'Hey...'

Before I could speak, he turns on his heels and leaves, walking swiftly towards a shack that is probably his quarters.

I consider chasing him, but the rain is getting harder. I think of the snakes that sneak up in the night and shudder, picturing for a fleeting moment what Mamma must have endured the night the snakes had run riot somewhere on these banks. The sharp, impaling rain only adds to the goose bumps of dread the thought evoked in me.

Back in my room in the ashram, I read Mamma's diary all over again. With less dread now than in the initial days of its finding. I remember the first time I had read it after I chanced upon it, years after she died. I should have discovered it earlier, but my reluctance to rummage through her belongings kept many of her secrets intact.

I avoided every single thing that reminded me of her. It was part guilt and part grief. I knew that if not for my confrontation with her that day, she might have lived longer. Albeit with the weight of her woes. What expedited her exit was my rude rejection of her the day I knew that the river story was concocted. For this, I shall never forgive myself.

This trip, in some ways, is my way of atoning for the grave error of not realising the truth behind Mamma's compulsion to weave a river story for me. It will rinse my guilt. As for the grief, it will stay. Beyond my grave even. It is raining relentlessly outside. This part of the ashram is more of an inn for visitors to stay than a centre for any spiritual activity. Most places that aren't visibly hotels are called ashrams here. It ascribes a certain saintly distinction to the lodging space, a sense of safety to those who come calling from faraway places. Women who travel solo have found them to be a refuge where the fangs of nightly creatures can't reach.

I can't stop thinking of the snakes that the watchman spoke about. I know he wasn't lying. They infest the dark nights here.

It isn't that there aren't snakes lurking around during the day in places around the river. There are, but they don't bare their fangs. They cleverly conceal their diabolical nature. They befriend gullible creatures, and in the most unsuspecting moment, bite.

There is a page in the diary that I have stuck a bookmark into. I flick the page open—its content by now memorised. Then I leaf through the pages that follow. It is where my life has remained stuck ever since I discovered the diary.

Every time I run my eyes through Mamma's writing in those pages, I feel my body stiffen. I hold my breath and heave loudly. Initially, it made me run to the sink and throw up. I voluntarily undergo this unpleasantness to feel the pain vicariously. I do it so that my obligation towards Mamma isn't forgotten. I punish myself this way for letting her die.

At dinner time, I go to the common hall, but find the sight of food unappetising. I serve myself some rice and dal and pretend to eat, all the while glancing around the hall, sizing up the people from the kitchen who flitted in and out carrying out their duties, and giving the few guests present a cursory glance.

I evinced a particular interest in them all, not being of their sort. Even though westerners are a common sight here, I do not look like the ones who come here seeking nirvana, distinct by their dreadlocks, piercings, and ragtag attire. There is nothing rumpled about me, and this made me even more a subject of interest.

'Madam, some rice?' a middle-aged guy from the kitchen comes sounding solicitous.

I say 'no' by shaking my head. I knew he expected me to smile, and I oblige grudgingly. It must have made his day. I find his manner slimy but it is something I have come to terms with, although it is supremely revolting. Men in this country have a bit of a thing for the white skin.

Earlier in the day, when I was spending the afternoon by the ghat, two men, probably in their late twenties, approached me asking to take a picture with me. Clad in jeans and chequered shirts, both had religious tattoos inked on their arms. They were men who carried Gods on their sleeves.

'We want a photo with you, please,' said one and sidled next to me, cloyingly.

Even before I could react, by consent or rejection, I had the two men flanking me, hands on my shoulders. One of them flashed his smart phone up, while the other squeezed into the frame, his hand pressing into my shoulder, and I only remember staring into the camera, bewildered. Behind me in the frame, a stray bull calf was chewing on an abandoned food packet.

My first instinct was to punch the men in their eye for violating my space, but I restrained myself, I didn't want to attract attention by creating any ruckus. I sprang to my feet shaking, and merely yelled, 'What do you think you are doing? Who gave you the permission to take my picture with you?'

'We just took a picture with you. We do it with tourists here all the time,' one of the two men said with a random flick of his hand. 'And we know you firangis don't mind it,' he added, sneering viciously and trotting off.

Firangis. Foreigners. I have read this word in Mamma's diary. That's how they had referred to her too. I find the word very derogatory. Cheap. It made me feel as if it gave them the privilege to mess with us as they pleased, because in their view we were easy. 'Firangis don't mind it.'

I wanted to tell them that I minded, that I felt grossly dishonoured when they put their hand on me for their momentary pleasure which they would later flaunt among their friends.

I felt like throwing up into the river but I just sank to the ground. The river is sacred to me and I couldn't sully it. It was my father for a long time which by traditional Indian belief is an anomaly. To the countless millions in this country, the river was a woman. And a woman cannot produce a child with another woman. I should have known it.

For all the despise I have for the man who ogles and leers at me in the dining hall, I give him a soppy smile every time he comes around checking on me. He seems to be among the oldest members in the kitchen, and if my estimate turns out to be right, he might have been here on that day twenty-three years ago. It is only a possibility that I am considering, not a conviction. It would help to befriend him. He could give me clues.

'The food here is tasty,' I say, when he accosts me with his foolish face at dinner again.

'I am the head cook,' he says, proudly. 'Especially appointed by Swamiji. I have been cooking for his devotees and guests for twenty-five years now.'

'Twenty-five years? And appointed by Swamiji? Why, you must be quite an expert,' I feign my appreciation and slurp a spoonful of dal.

'How many days' stay, madam?' The man asks sticking his head forward eagerly.

I briefly look away miffed by his grotesque grin and return to answer him. Who knows what thoughts the imaginations of these men are made of? Nonetheless, he could be useful.

'A few days,' I say and quickly add, 'I want a favour, er...I didn't ask your name.'

'Kishen...Kishen.'

There is something about the name that disconcerts me. A familiarity. I make a mental note of his name.

'Kishen-Kishen. Twice?' I ask just to humour him. 'You are very funny, madam,' he says scratching his head self-consciously. 'But you are very nice. I like you. What can I do for you?'

Who in this place doesn't like our white-skinned sort, the thought filled me with loathing. Instead, I ask, 'Have you really been here for that many years?'

'Yes. Swamiji hasn't let me go from here. I came here as a trainee cook, now I head this kitchen.'

'It is almost like you have become part of its history.

You will be knowing quite a lot about this place then.

Will you take me around, and may be even take me to meet the Swamiji?

'Anything for you, madam.'

I couldn't stand the man's fizzy enthusiasm to please me. The fact that he looked past middle-age and had grey hair was in direct incongruence with his manner that had a layer of licentiousness beneath it.

'Swamiji doesn't give private audience very easily. But he would, if I say. I am close to him, a humble servant of twenty-five years.'

'Thank you, Kishen-Kishen. That would be very kind of you. I have come here all the way to meet him. My greatest wish. I know he brings lasting peace to people's lives with a single glance,' I said grabbing his hand in mock gratitude. The physical contact was sufficient for Kishen to promise me that he would arrange for it as soon as possible.

'People say He is God, madam, capable of giving people the ultimate moksha,' Kishen says touching his ear and closing his eyes in reverence.

In the evening, I amble out to the riverbank, and watch small groups of devotees float their flickering lamps in the gushing monsoon river, waiting for them to gain speed and merge with the holy waters. Some lamps die out early, some get swept into the whirlpools and sink, and only some make it to the farther reaches of the stream. Yet they all indulge in the ritual, braving the uncertainty, watching it till their eyes can see, for it symbolised life's vagaries to them.

A few metres away from where I sit is a row of cottages in the middle of a garden. It is the abode of the holy man. The prospect of meeting him excites me in a strange, evil way. Soon, I will find my redemption, attain moksha, that which devout Hindus do years and years of penance for. I have done my penance too, gone through my period of suffering, living through the aftermath of Mamma's death, the revelation of her past and the ugly truth about my origin.

The monsoon clouds are gathering in the sky and the rain is waiting at the threshold of the twilight. Pilgrims are undaunted, as they take their holy dips in the cold river and float their wishes into the yonder. The river is always cold. Nonchalant. It barely stops to take note of the men and women who come to it to brazenly dump their sins. It is as if their debauchery can barely touch its soul. So, all the scum that it is loaded with goes without sullying it.

It reminds me of a line that I keep returning to in Mamma's diary. 'This body is not yours. Only the spirit is yours. So, let go off your body. Let go off your body.'

Which is what she did, eventually. Not when she let her body be used as a rag, but when she let the blood in it seep out on her pink, embroidered bedspread.

I hatefully think of the man who had taught her that irrational maxim twenty-three years ago. Somewhere among the trees, in one of those sprawling buildings, he must have indoctrinated her. Given her the quick fix to her woes with his rotting pontification.

I imagine the diabolic words he must have used in the end to invade her. I see him pinning her down with his nasty hands that he raises dramatically to bless people with in public.

I see Mamma's white, lamb-like face, fraught with fear and helplessness. She had come to him of her own volition, to escape the pain of a different sort, and then, this.

'All the pain is because you think this body is yours. This body is not yours. It is mine, your divine reliever. Give it to me and you will know no more pain. Give it to me,' the snake in the holy garb must have hissed into her ears.

Or did he and his lecherous mates who were waiting for their turn not even speak of her body, but ripped it apart till she had nothing left of her own to give them?

I begin to pant and shutting my eyes tight, I scream inwardly.

As darkness fell, I see people slowly leaving, content in the thought that they were purified for now. They can now go back to their vices, and when its weight gets insufferable, return to dump the filth in the ever- accepting river. They know, the river will always pardon its prodigal children.

The cold air and the drizzle make me want to take shelter, but I waver by the banks for a while before putting my feet into the water and slowly descending in it to take a dip. I rise, scalded by the chillness, and then in a frenzied impulse dip again. And then again. And again. Till Mamma's screams merge with my inner cry, and together they dissolve in the downward stream.

In the morning, at the breakfast table, Kishen has good news for me.

'Swamiji is in silence for two days. However, he has consented to meet you soon after that. I said to him that you intend to join the congregation and work closely with him.'

I begin to protest, but Kishen raises his hand and says, 'That is just to win him over. A request for a casual meeting is never accepted. I added it from my side for your sake,' he winks and vindicates his lie.

I admire his ingenuity and thank him in the mind for making my access to the Swamiji easy. I am beginning to feel an evil elation at the proximity of a dream coming true.

'Do a lot of people join him, Kishen, leaving their homes and livelihood?' I ask, breaking a slice of bread and dipping it into the milky tea in a typical Indian rustic manner. Mamma used to like untoasted bread dipped in milky tea, I remember. A taste she had developed here and carried back home.

'Hordes of people are part of his social and spiritual work, but only a few are taken into his core team. The rest are followers, devotees. Coming and going.'

'So, what will I be, if I were to join the congregation?'

'Why, part of his core team, of course. He believes that people like you are an asset to him. You will take his message to the west and propagate his teachings. Truth be told, Indians have lost all faith in their philosophy. They have become deviant. The west has more respect for our ancient teachings.'

'Boy, am I lucky to be in Swamiji's core team even without asking for it!'

'I recommended for you, madam, because you are very good to me,' Kishen says flashing his pan-stained teeth once again in a foolish smile.

'Thank you, Kishen.' I pat his palm that was resting lightly on the table and let it stay there for an extra moment than I had desired. It was to return his favour. I notice the ugly warts on his fingers and flinch. Kishen raises his other hand as if to put it on mine, but retreats when I suddenly rise to my feet to go.

I resist the temptation to talk to Kishen about a firangi woman who had come to the ashram twenty-three years ago. I wonder if he would know or remember. How many firangis the snake must have taken into his fold since then and converted them to voiceless, body- less willows?

Two days can be a long time when one is waiting for uncertainty. The rains have been ruthless and it keeps me indoors. I stare at the window for long and imagine that I could become the river, swell and swallow this land along with its snakes. I open my journal.

'Tonight, I want to become the murderous waters that can wipe everything out. Every memory. Every trace of the past. Every residue of evil. Every whimper of women. Every stain that their tears must have left on earth's surface.'

I open the window slightly and peer through to see the smudged flicker of lights in Swamiji's cluster. The flood waters inside me rise as I reach for Mamma's diary. I read a few pages with fire in my eyes. My eyes pause in the middle, struck by a familiar name. I circle it with a shivering finger. A repulsive mass of warts and a toothy smile flash before my eyes and I dig my face in the pillow and cry loud and deep into it.

How many were there on that day? I don't know. All I know is that a pack of hyenas feasted on the flesh left behind by a satiated head beast.

Mamma fled this place a day later. The biggest mistake she did was that she never told her story to anyone. And for that, I will never forgive her. I will never forgive her for living with the stigma of her story and for dying with its burden.

Sometime in the middle of the night, over the noise of the river in full spate, I hear a faint knock on the door.

It is Kishen.

'Madam, I have something to tell you,' he whispers urgently through the door that I held slightly ajar.

I feel a sudden instinct to slam the door shut, but before I could, he slides in through the door and shuts it behind him.

'Stay away from me,' I say suddenly, and reach for something to hurl at him.

I don't find anything on the table except Mamma's diary. I fling the book at him. He catches it in time, advances towards me and says urgently, 'I have an important message from Swamiji.'

'Kishen, do you know I could kill you now and no one would know?' I tell him menacingly. I know what I had just said was mistimed and I didn't mean it, but it was all I could do to cover my fear.

I see Kishen's face turn grey under the tube light.

Night insects of different sizes are swarming in abandon under the fluorescent tube as if it was their last night of orgy. Soon, they will fall to their death, their wings severed from their bodies. The bodies that aren't theirs. Did they know that philosophy?

'Have you gone mad?' Kishen backs off as I find an iron door latch on the windowsill and grab it. 'I came to tell you that....'

'Don't pretend, you dirty old urchin! You didn't come here to say anything. You came here to destroy me the way you destroyed my mamma. You...scorpions and snakes...you thought no one would find out.'

I suddenly taste blood in my mouth and realise that I was biting my lips hard while I hollered my wrath on the intruder in my room. I swipe my forearm on my lips and hurl the latch at him. Kishen ducks and the missile lands on the door behind him.

The rain outside pounds harder and muffles the commotion in my room. I am appalled to see that Kishen is making no attempt to escape. I have provoked him and he reveals his hideous form. He bares his fangs, pounces on me, pushing me down with his warty hands. I stagger and fall backwards, and land on the floor. A sense of déjà vu flashes in my scrambled head.

I shut my eyes in horror and feel my body convulse as the repulsive smell of Kishen's sweat seeps in and makes me nauseous. I scream from the pit of my stomach, 'No, you will not do to me what you did to my mamma and others after her.'

I bite his hand hard and push him with all my might. I am surprised at the force I could summon into my arms. He lurches and lands on his back, and before he can stand on his feet again, I get up, run to the bathroom and pick up the heavy steel pail under the tap.

In less than two minutes, I see the crushed skull of Kishen on the floor, a river of red winding down the mosaic tiles. I stuff my things in my duffle bag and before I flee, I spit at the bloodied face of the vermin who might have been my father.

Then I begin to run. Out into the lancing rain and dead night. There are snakes still lurking here. Lording over them is a king cobra that people worship as god. Before the damned god can get me, I must escape.

I sprint through the dark, narrow, water-logged lanes.

I know I cannot stop. I cannot die. I am a river child. I run, knowing my moksha is still a long way away.

CHAPTER EIGHT

DISTRESSED JEANS

'Mini, your mom is a star now. She is all over the media. Did you see it? It took so long for me to realise how glamorous she is indeed!' my daughter's father said scooping a ladle of what he described as the best ever chicken curry in the world.

I remember the first time he had tasted it, soon after our wedding forty-nine years ago. He ate a mouthful, licked his fingers unabashedly and then looked at me from across the table and smiled. And then, another mouthful and a smile. It was all he could do to convey his appreciation in the presence of his parents and family. To a new bride, his relish meant reassurance. Nothing could have made life worthy for her than to know that she had found the way to her man's heart with a chicken curry.

The way that was paved that day to his life's centre has not closed ever since. A knowing glance and a profound smile became the hallmarks of his minimalist expressions of appreciation in public. And I sought it every time out of the corner of my eye, as I did today. That I am sixty-nine and he seventy-five is beside the point.

'Appa, do you really think it was required? Did she have to do this?' Mini expressed her disappointment making sure that her glance didn't meet mine. 'Do you know what my friends think?'

'That you have a sexy mother?' Mini's Appa joked and winked at me.

I was appalled that he had used that word to describe me to Mini, but deep down it tickled me and I shook my head in mock dismay.

'Appa!' Mini exclaimed. 'I don't believe you are so cool about what has happened. It's your wife, my mother that the whole world is discussing in such unpleasant terms.'

I quietly sat watching Mini hold a trial against me for a decision I had made on a whim. She had already expressed her outrage to me over phone in no uncertain terms. She wasn't alarmed that her father hadn't raise a brow. What upset her was that I wasn't prudent enough to know that it wasn't okay for a sixty-nine-year-old woman to wear distressed jeans and look glamorous on social media.

According to her, after five decades of making the world's best chicken curry, I was seeking out cheap popularity by doing unconventional things. She was appalled that I had allowed myself to cross the limits and made a caricature of myself in front of people. That she had to explain it to her folks, including her in laws.

'Appa, it's not funny. Why did she have to do it at this age? Couldn't you stop her?'

'Why should I stop her now when I haven't done it all these years? And by the way, I really thought she looked good in the trendy clothes that she wore in those pictures.' He grinned, infuriating Mini further.

How different a smile can look with dentures, I thought. I was grateful that the cosmetic changes apart, everything was intact between us. He stuck up for me even when our daughter disapproved my ways, not so much because it bothered her personally perhaps, but because she had to answer people and mollify their concerns.

'Do you have any idea what people are talking about her, what kinds of comments are being posted?' Mini thundered.

I spooned myself some rice and cleared my throat to express my displeasure at the way she spiked her voice, but Mini didn't seem to care. Appa's pet was on a rampage today and although I was the cause of the rage, I was not inclined to explain, justify or pacify her, for I wasn't guilty of my act.

'Take some more rice,' I said to Mini, deliberately breaking her spiel. She waved my offer away and turned to her father again.

'Appa, I am speaking to you. Oh God, what has come over my parents? Why don't they see what the whole world sees?'

'What does the whole world see, Mini?' I asked gently, reaching over and serving some rice in her father's plate.

'How much will you feed me? I am stuffed already. But if you insist...,' he said and mixed the rice with some curry.

'Yes, so what is the world seeing that your mother and I are not?' Mini's Appa asked.

Mini got up in a huff, fished her phone from her bag and scrolling up and down, presented to her father a stream of responses to my pictures on Facebook. They were mean, reprehensible, and deeply misogynistic, I must admit. Some were downright vulgar and rude, and I was glad Mini's father didn't have a Facebook account of his own to discover the monstrosities of a new age. He saw only what I showed him, and I had carefully kept the rotten remarks out of his sight.

'Read this, Appa,' Mini said thrusting the phone in his hand.

She didn't have to do it for whatever good reason it was, I lamented in my heart. I waited to see her Appa's expression as he slowly read each comment, his brows arching up when he stumbled upon a happy one and furrowing when a toxic one showed up.

'Did you read this?' he suddenly said and started laughing. 'Can I adopt you, beautiful grandma? My dadi doesn't allow me to wear ripped jeans or western clothes. Will you be my grandma?'

'You are in great demand, all said,' he declared.

I beamed wide and shook my head.

He then handed the phone to Mini and said, 'Well, it takes all kinds to make the world. I think we have to make a choice as to where we belong. We can be kind or mean. Where do you choose to be, Mini?'

My heart fluttered and eyes stung with gratitude. He must have given me the chicken-curry smile then, but overwhelmed with emotion, I turned away.

'What did your mother do? Dress up in modern clothes and do a photoshoot. She has always been a stunning woman, Mini, elegant and royal. Didn't the pictures do justice to her?'

And after a pause he asked, 'How many selfies do you and Shruti post for people to see in a week? Has she ever questioned you about it?'

Shruti is our eighteen-year-old granddaughter.

'How can you compare the two of us with her, Appa?

Consider our ages, please,' Mini retorted.

'Amma is sixty-nine, you are forty-five. She is young and vibrant, with a zest for life, making the best chicken curry in the world. You are shrunk and caught up in the narrowness of the world, influenced by strangers and knocked around by others. Do you know why, despite being her daughter, you don't make chicken curry like she does even after all these years? It's because you never wanted to adopt the good things from her. You just indiscriminately picked up what others had to teach you. And today, you are turning against the very person who brought you up.'

Mini's face turned rufous. I wished her father didn't say anything more. I rose, walked towards Mini, and put a hand on her shoulder. I felt her stiffen under my touch. 'What is it that bothers you, Mini? That I look good at my age and live a life of my choice? Or that your father allows me more freedom than what your husband allows you? Or the fact that a section of our society considers it blasphemous and so, you disapprove it too? Or are you seriously ashamed of your mother?' I asked without raising my voice.

'It's what people are writing about you. Calling you names, humiliating you. I can't tolerate all of that. You didn't need to go through it, Amma. Not at this age. You have had an honourable life all these years. Why did you have to thwart it now by posing for a few photographs that is unbecoming of your age or stature? Are you not hurt that people are heaping abuses on you?'

I forced a smile, squeezed her shoulder once and whispered, 'Do you know what pained me the most? That my daughter didn't stand by me when she should have been among the first to speak up for me. That my own off spring fell to bigotry. That she made me look like an errant child. Mini, we didn't raise you this way. Where did we go wrong, Mini's Appa?'

I was careful not to sound apologetic, not even to my daughter, but I couldn't hide my despair.

An uneasy silence seeped into our midst as he finished his dinner and on his way to the sink tapped my arm twice as if to calm me.

I don't know why, but I expected Mini to respond, or at least show a hint of remorse in her face. Perhaps, she had expected the same of me too. An obstinate mother could have begotten only a defiant daughter.

It seemed unlikely that she was going to be assuaged, and I saw no need to offer her any comfort either. Those who were inflamed by my life will find their own salve, and that would include my daughter too.

'Amma, can you do me a favour? Can you please write a post that will bury this for good, and...take your photos down? And please, if you want to be in the

limelight, do it in a way that doesn't bring us all shame. I live in a joint family, for God's sake.'

I laughed loud and rejected her proposal almost instantly. Taking the pictures down was out of question. A follow-up post could be considered. I conveyed my thoughts to her and said it was up to her to either take pride in her mother or be ashamed of her. She had a choice to applaud her mother for standing out or hide in a closet with embarrassment or even disown her if that would bring her peace. All these because I was different from other senior citizens she had known in her life. It is an irony that the one she had to know the closest was the one she knew the least.

'Mini, remember this. I gave birth to you and not vice versa,' I said a tad coldly before she left, to remind her that I was in charge of my life, and not her.

Later that night, after Mini's Appa had gone to sleep, I pulled out my letter pad and began to write. I had promised to write a follow-up post.

My dear daughter, (and all others who hated me for living life on my terms),

First, thank you for making me famous. For close to seven decades, I have lived a relatively anonymous life, happy within my confines, doing the things that made me and my family happy. I have always heard that the twilight years were a drag. They were accompanied by aching knees, dimming vision, foggy memory, and above all, savage boredom.

I had started waiting for these things to afflict me the day I turned 60 because that's what I believed the law of life dictated. But guess what? Even as the limbs began to slow down, the spirit remained intact, as sprightly as a teen's. Life, instead of winding down, gained momentum once I retired from service. I found myself opening up to a myriad of things to do and spend the rest of my life. That I had the whole-hearted support of my spouse in whatever I did in my life was an added advantage to me. God bless his good heart.

The first thing I did after I hit sixty was to stop colouring my hair, not because I didn't have the need to look younger, but because I felt the salt and pepper look added glamour to my greying years. I loved the sense of freedom and confidence looking good at sixty brought me. It's a blessing to feel beautiful at that age. For reasons I have never been able to fathom, the older one got, the less significant looking good became. It still baffles me why. It's in the autumn season that the leaves look pretty, don't they? Does the tree condemn the beauty of its foliage at that time?

The next thing I did was to resolve that I would not take post-retirement lessons from others of my age. It had nothing to do with what they did, but I realised that each had their own way of justifying their time on this planet, and I wanted to chart my own course without influences. I allowed them their choices, and I expected them not to interfere in mine.

I had a number of unfulfilled dreams stacked up in my kitty. From little things like growing a balcony garden to learning to cycle to moderate things like wanting to learn art to fairly ambitious things like taking

up an acting course and joining a theatre group. Suddenly, with all the leisure in the world, I felt like I owned all the field to play my shots with gay abandon.

All the while, so many of you were conspiring against me in devious ways, to thwart my joys, to curb my space, to make me fit in stereotyped closets of old age, weren't you?

There can be several irrational motives behind someone throwing cold water on others' lives; I do not know what yours was, but if it has brought you satisfaction and made your life better, I am happy. Like your mother or grandmother would be.

As someone who has seen a lot more life than you all might have seen, I have only this to say. I do not know how many years are left of my life, but whatever remains of it, I intend to varnish it with positive, vibrant paints. I refuse to become a fossil while alive. And after death, I want flowers to be planted on my grave to remind people that beneath the earth my soul still thrives.

I invite you with no malice or rancour in my heart to join in my celebration of life, or if it still rankles you that at sixty-nine, I look a lot happier, freer, and more at peace than you, let me say—it is not too late. Sow the right seeds now so that you will reap a rich harvest as time passes by.

How we spend our old age is something we must all reflect upon when we are younger. How we fashion our thoughts in our prime is what will decide the nature of our advancing years. It is not about what life will give you, but what you will give back to life that makes the difference. A lot of muck and dirt is the last thing we would want to carry on our backs to the kingdom of peace.

I owe no explanation to anyone for the things I do in my life for I mean no harm to anyone. It's to no one's detriment. I am merely living my life to the fullest, and I wish you will too.

God bless. I remain. xxx'

I folded the sheet in half, held it for a few moments and with deep deliberation, tore it through the middle. I made a few more pieces of it and deposited it in the dust bin in the corner of the room. I snuggled into the blanket after turning the lights off, closed my eyes, and said my prayer as the soft purrs of Mini's Appa snoring, swept over me.

'Life hasn't been perfect, Lord, but if you were to give me a chance to live all over again, I wouldn't want you to change a thing. Thank you, for everything.'

CHAPTER NINE

FREE SPIRIT

It is seven in the evening, and I drag myself lazily out of bed. The day light is receding from the room and the silence is acquiring a rare quality. The three men who share the room with me are still away at work. The grogginess irritates me and the pangs of hunger gnaw at my intestines. I let the air of emptiness from the stomach escape with a glass of water. I call it the burp of the famished man stuffed to neck with hunger.

Like a nocturnal creature eager to break free into the familiarity of darkness, I prepare for my outing in the city – circuits around the parking lot of the hyper market. At the end of that sojourn, I would have a few rials in my pocket. Then a leisurely stroll to the coffee shop where I would lounge till the shop shut well past midnight. A shawarma sandwich and a cup of tea would impatiently tear into my stomach, giving it the long- awaited solace.

This has been my routine for the evenings since the time I became this moron that people have come to refer me as.

Moron. Vagabond, and much before that, 'good for nothing', as my father used to call me. Over time I have gathered more such epithets, none too complimentary.

I trundled out, slipping across my shoulder the sling bag stuffed with inexpensive Chinese toys. The bag rested primly on my side as if happy and content to be where it belonged. It is strange that every little thing in the world feels the need to belong and stay. Why then had I become such a drifter in soul, spirit and body? Why then was I such an aberration, mindless of everything except the craving to exist in whatever condition. Even as a 'good for nothing'.

Perhaps I wasn't so earlier, when I was a little more than a boy. Yet in my father's estimate, I was a good for nothing offspring that should never have happened in the first place.

But I had happened and so, I had to be kept.

I have never enquired what it was that he required of me. If it was academics, I wasn't cut out for it. If it was restrained habits, I was past the stage of correction. I wasn't completely incorrigible but I was beyond the stage where my father could get me to conform to his dictates. I had somehow grown up to be reckless and wayward. That was the way I was and still am. Moron. Vagabond. Good for nothing.

It was a gross miscalculation on my father's part to expect that his effort to make me temperate would have any desired effect on me, for I grew more indignant and vagrant in my ways. It was just the way I had happened. I worked and paid for my own personal needs and pleasure. And that, I believed, was the way to exist. My people were just peripherals. It wasn't my fault that there were three girls in the family, it wasn't my fault that their marriage meant dowry and debt, it wasn't my fault that father's health began to deteriorate and it wasn't my fault that a farm labourer had mighty, unrealistic expectations of his only son.

One day, intimidated by the burdens that waited to fall on me, I left, leaving a note. It was futile to pin hopes on me, I scribbled. I wanted to live life on my terms. I wanted freedom. I do not remember if I tagged a word of apology with it. Not one for mushiness and emotions, it was unlikely that I did. I don't think such pretences would have mattered much either.

I rarely thought about what must have transpired in the family in the wake of my departure. They must have probably taken it in their stride, knowing me to be one that couldn't be looked up to even in the direst of circumstances. In a way, it was good that I had carved a poor reputation for myself. It might have helped them come to terms with my exit and helped them to consign me to a forgettable past with less agony. Gone. Dead for all practical purposes.

Believe me or not, I rarely reflect on my past. I am inherently a man of the present, but today, memories are occurring relentlessly and for some reason, I find myself incapable of fighting them. So, I let them hang about me, like the humid summer air.

Being sober (as I am now) has its own deficiencies. I hate the clarity of thought that prevails in this state. It makes me reflective and nostalgic, in a manner that being sozzled doesn't. The two states are distinguished by a sense of remorse that stabs at me when I am not drunk. The awareness of being good for nothing emerges and torments me until it is doused by some brandy. So, I keep myself in a constant state of drunken delirium, preferably.

Like in the past, I manage to find money for my daily habits and pleasures. I have a freelance job as a handy man and then there is my sales outings. Although, put together, my engagements fetch me barely enough for my food, shelter and drinks. On days when there isn't enough, I beg and borrow from my roommates who hand out a pittance grudgingly. They tolerate me only because like me they too are staying illegally in this country. The common fear of being tracked down keeps us together as a cluster despite our differences and grievances.

It is with dread that I think of a raid by the police. Being caught is presently my greatest fear in life. It meant not just a prison term but also deportation to my homeland at the end of the term, and going back home is the one thing I never want to do in my life. I had left it once, swearing never to return unless I had amassed enough wealth and dignity to obliterate the tags conferred on me by my family.

Twenty-three years on, I am where I was—still doing odd jobs for my subsistence and small pleasures. There is nothing illustrious about my life that I can display. Yet I continue to live because I love this life of a drifter. Free from care, devoid of responsibility, unattached, unsought, it is the life of a bird. My attachments have been fleeting, love has been non-existent, and associations have been convenience driven. I am not answerable to any authority, neither indebted to anyone's largesse nor responsible for anyone's life save my own. There are no emotional strings that tug at my heart and I like it this way.

I sometimes wonder if this was the kind of life that yogis led. If they did, then I am nothing less than a yogi. It is a curious thought, and it often makes me chuckle mischievously. The yogi who drinks, sleeps with whores (when there is money), and saunters around in a state of stupor!

I am amused that people find my aimlessness gross and intolerable. They despise my strutting around, drowned in liquor. People who know me well suggest that I either reform or commit suicide. People who don't know me see me from far and change their path.

Only the other day, when I asked Mustafa for some money that he said, 'Why don't you go and die? For whom do you live this way?'

Having got used to such frequent remonstrations, I had no malice towards him even when he spewed anger. 'I don't think I have a reason to die, not now at least.' My words incensed him further.

'Tell me one thing. Why do you live?' Mustafa asked, peering into my face with seething rage.

'You tell me, why should I die? I am pleased with the way I live.' I answered before taking the last swig with a vicious smile.

Thinking about this whole business of 'going and dying', I must admit that there was a time when I had thought that suicide was a good way to escape wretchedness. In the long years that I have been here in

the Middle East, I have seen men of many kinds: from the excessively rich to the pathetically deprived. There were those who changed cars and those who changed wives like they changed cars; those who behaved like animal tamers and those who yielded like fallen soldiers. The motley that I have come across often made me laugh; the world was such an amusing pack of playing cards. There were clowns of all kinds in it.

The fallen soldiers were the ones I knew the most and the best. The besieged lot of human beings who cried in joy and laughed in sorrow. Many, who had become mere machines, or worse, oxen that ceaselessly ploughed their dreary lives for the sake of others—parents, wife, children and siblings.

I pitied them for their over-burdened existence, constantly striving to fulfil someone else's need in the name of love and obligation. They inflated themselves so much with compulsions that they eventually popped out, leaving a suicide note, or sometimes leaving only a stunning silence of disbelief among those left around. To many, it was the only way of redemption from the pressures of a lifetime.

Take Saravanan for example, the man who served at the restaurant. He was found hanging from the ceiling of his room only a day after he spoke to his friends of his desire to go home on a vacation. He was only twenty-seven. It was impossible to imagine that behind his serene exteriors there was a sinister plan. To think that it was playing on his mind when he served me tea in the restaurant that evening and then came down to ask if I could lend him some money. I was amused that he had into my empty shirt pocket.

All that I knew about Saravanan was that he was saddled with immense responsibilities and debts. But that was how the fallen soldiers lived—mired in wretchedness—and it was commonplace. It was only when things went overboard, beyond ordinary levels of endurance that people left suicide notes. I wonder if Saravanan had come to that point so early in life.

A day after it took place, I went to the restaurant to gather details. Raja, his roommate, said as he put my tea on the table, 'Committing suicide is the worst thing a man can do to those he leaves behind. It is the most selfish thing to do.'

'He must have had compulsions,' I said, bleakly.

'What compulsions?' Raja said, furiously. 'Who among us doesn't have money problems? Who doesn't miss home? Whoever in this place is happy? Does everyone go and hang?'

I had no answer. But I was certain that Saravanan had a compelling reason. Everyone who did it had a reason and I told him that.

'You are talking about reasons? I can give you a hundred reasons why you and I should go and do it too. Not finding money for your daily booze can be a reason to you. Not being able to fulfil my family's big dreams can be a reason to me. The man out there can do it if he lost his job. The students in the school can do it if the teacher caned them or yelled at them. Who doesn't have a reason?'

Yes, who doesn't have a reason, except perhaps me? I didn't tell him that, for in his estimation everyone in this world had a reason to go and hang, if he wanted to, that is.

In my case, it is just that I simply didn't want to do it. I am pleased with the way I live and I don't care if it made anyone else's life less happy. I thought of Mustafa and his frequent rants over me.

'Poor guy,' I whispered, unconsciously.

'Who is the poor guy?' Raja thundered. 'He deserves no sympathy. Forget about the fact that he owed us all so much money. Did he think of his family that banked on him so heavily? He did such an unforgivable act. It is sheer betrayal.'

I merely nodded as if to agree.

What a grace that I didn't have a family to think and lose my sleep over!

'I will never do it,' I tell a disgruntled Mustafa time and again.

I know that Mustafa secretly admired my ability to hold my own despite all that I didn't have in life. No job, no relations, no dreams, nor regrets. I can sense the envy that he so discreetly wraps in rage and lobs at me time and again. Who in this world doesn't long to be a free spirit?

In the evening, I walk past an old graveyard on my way to the restaurant. It is a harsh reminder of what would befall one and all eventually, that it is the final resting place that one arrives at after fighting the battles of a lifetime.

A weird thought crosses my mind. If I were to come under the wheels of a speeding car someday when my luck runs out, this is the place I would be dumped in by the angels of the Municipality, unlike Saravanan who was flown home in a coffin to be received by grieving relatives.

There is something uniquely enchanting about these evenings that I spend at the restaurant. Sitting outside and watching TV even hours after I have paid for my food makes me feel doubly liberated. If there is some place in this world where I feel I belong, it is here. So indescribably cozy and satisfying even in this hot humid month of August that I felt even the stars above frown with envy!

Gangu, the crippled cat who has made the restaurant premises his realm, hops up to me and I throw a few crumbs which he sniffs before nibbling. I have often wondered if it was better for him to have died than to live as a cripple for life. If only cats could tell. I watch him munch the crumbs. Besides his name that someone gave him, he has another identity: cripple cat. Like me having epithets. It is a bizarre comparison, but I indulge in thoughts about Gangu and me.

'Who gave you this name?' I ask.

Gangu doesn't answer but I continue to talk and no one takes notice.

'How do you live without a limb? Why didn't you die in the accident that maimed you? Are you now happy to be a cripple cat?'

When the crumbs are finished, Gangu moves on, oblivious to my questions. Unsteady, untroubled and unsought, in many ways he replicated me.

The last of the local customers leave from a table adjacent to mine. I walk up and shuffle the channels and arrive at a Malayalam channel. I love watching these programs for the sheer nostalgia that they induce in me. My memories about Kerala rekindle and thoughts resurface as I watch sights that once were so familiar to me. The people and places that flash on the screen evoke a forgotten, latent desire. I don't get repentant, just reflective about a place that I may never see again. I yearn to reach out to the screen and touch them.

I rise to go after a while, heavy with disquiet when something on the TV catches my attention. I plunk back into the chair shaken by what I see. I peer at the TV screen with disbelief and horror, and close in to catch the details of a conversation.

A middle-aged woman is sitting next to an old, teary-eyed one while the host of the program listened to them, nodding and asking brief questions in between.

'How long is it since he left?'

'Twenty-seven years. He left one day and never returned,' said the old woman, sobbing. Words trickled from her toothless mouth and tears ran over the heavily wrinkled cheeks.

'Do you think he is still alive? Twenty-seven years is a very long time for anyone not to contact home unless he is dead.'

The harshness in the program host's statement pricks me but I look on. I feel weak in my knees and I sit again.

'His father believed that he would come back some day. He thought so till the day he died.'

When did he die?

'Did he ever write to you?' the man asks.

'For the first few months there was no letter. But one day we received a letter from him saying he was in the Gulf working for a company. He sent us money a few times. But that was years ago.'

The middle-aged woman is speaking now. She looks familiar but distant in memory, like a half-forgotten dream.

'He left home in anger for reasons we don't know. We thought he was playing pranks. But when he did not return even after days, our father fell sick and took to the bed. After two years of being bedridden, he died. It was his wish that we find him. Then someone told us about this program on TV that helped people trace missing relatives in the Gulf. We wanted to try one last time.'

She too has tears welling up.

'I only want to see him once before I die,' says the old woman, so shrivelled and weakened by time.

They flash a photograph on the screen. It bears no resemblance to my current appearance. It was preposterous that those people had such an old sketchy photograph as a reference. How can the frayed picture of an adolescent in school uniform help find a bald, messy, and middle-aged man after all these years?

I ran my hand uneasily over my pate and down the curls that touched the nape. I had no reason to look any better than what I did. I went to the hair cutting salon infrequently, shaved once a week, and had a few changes of clothes.

There was nothing appealing about the boy in the photograph either. My clownish appearance in it had drawn immense ridicule from my sisters who for some reason never had a class photo taken during the few years that they went to school.

How much I hated them then! I remember having nourished a desire to tear their new clothes to shreds or worse, on days when I felt intensely annoyed, to strangle them to death when they slept. But all I did to get even with them was to call them names and show gestures.

My going away from home was the ultimate act of revenge on my sisters, father, and to some extent my mother. In my view, she was a silent but potent partner in their actions against me.

I wonder who supported their lives in the absence of my father. I assume that my sisters must have been married off, hopefully to men who were unlike me. I had no malice towards them now to wish them ill. So, I hoped that they were well.

The man on the TV is making an appeal to me to return home for the sake of my sister and mother. I wonder what had happened to my other sister.

The man moves on next to warning that he has a network of people who could find men from anywhere in the Gulf. He is making me feel like a fugitive on the run. I loathe him for it.

I look at my mother and sister for the last time and rise to go. I realise with disgust that they waited for me to return even after all these years. Their despair stabs at me. I don't know if I am remorseful or angry.

Suddenly, my years of obscurity seemed to have been peeled off and I feel exposed. I feel the eyes of the world staring at me with despise. The stars are mocking at my sudden nakedness and the breeze is hooting in my ears. The drudgery of life suddenly weighs down on me and I trudge on uncertainly.

Gradually, the night slows down to a stillness that soothes. I saunter on with only the city lights for company.

I hear the roar of the waves at a distance. The sea is in celebration. I walk towards it in a trance, eager to partake in its revelry. I pause at the fringes of the rampant, frolicking waves, wondering if I was welcome to their party. But fervent as ever, they come rolling, washing my feet, and ushering me in.

I coast into their midst warily. The city lights blur at a distance. I close my eyes and drift away.

CHAPTER TEN

SANTOS

It is two months since Juni left.

It must have been in a moment of utter weakness that I allowed her to leave. Or escape—from the problems she had created for herself, and in her wake, for me. Things had seemed urgent then, and if anyone could have helped her out of the deep trouble, she had found herself in, it was me.

I thought it was an opportunity to repay a debt. She had, after all, given me a life here and my folks back home a semblance of abundance in their lives. It was only after I came here that Joie and Chris started going to school, Dad and Mom got their long pending cataract operation done and my youngest one, three-year-old Sammy, got his first soft toy. A furry dog that blinked and stuck its tongue out every time he pressed a button in its belly.

Most of the good things in my life came because of Juni, including the Ray Ban glares, a pair that I coveted every time an overseas worker came home on vacation. Even my first date after divorce was set up by Juni a few weeks after I landed here, because according to her, every heart needed a good reason to beat. I owed a lot to Juni and the decision to help her somehow seemed like a way of paying back. But whoever knew that it would all end up this way?

'I have missed my periods,' she announced one day, flinging her bag on the bed and slumping wearily. We shared a room in a large apartment.

I stared at her trying to make sense.

'Atey, you mean...?

'I think so. I have to buy the kit and confirm.'

I panicked, but Juni showed no apprehension. How on earth could she be this careless?

I had wanted to know who it was, but in keeping with our unspoken agreement to not pry into each other's private lives, I held my tongue. It could have been anyone, given that we serviced all kinds of rich men-Arabs, Asians, and even Westerners-for making money on the side. It is illegal in this part of the world, but many things are glossed over because the standards of morality are fluid in a place that is as wealthy as this. Money can buy anything and anyone over.

'What will you do now?' I asked, weighing the options in my head. We weren't even in our home country. We were mere residents with work visas. Part of a fluid population. In a place like this, where we led regulated lives dictated by strict laws, it was impossible to get an abortion done.

What then?

Juni came and sat next to me. She was several years senior to me. I called her Atey, meaning sister. She looked old for her forty-five years. Her jaw bones had begun to show, there were purple moons under her eyes and even wrinkles had started to appear faintly. She always wore make-up to conceal the age. She had a particular penchant for hair colour, which she kept changing every few months. Her hair now had fluorescent green streaks, and they made her look sultry and desirable.

'This is my love-child. Not a bastard. Not conceived of someone unknown...randy prick.' Her words were measured and filled with emotion.

She opened a packet of corn curls and munched them slowly and purposefully as if she was contemplating something deep. She put it out to me lazily, but I declined. I had bile forming in my stomach. It almost felt as if I had missed my own period. The idea that it could happen to me too, although not likely considering how I insisted on condoms without compromise, made my heart leap.

'Love-child?'

'Yes, from Joshua.'

I was gob smacked. Joshua was the first man I had dated here. He was from the same village in Philippines as Juni and I. We went around together for a few months, and when we had exhausted our latent desires, we spent time talking of insignificant things. After a few months we called it quits, because there was nothing left for us to do with each other. Not even have sex. Most love affairs here don't have a direction. They are good while they last. Juni called them 'hook ups.' I called them 'picnics.'

'Were you and Joshua in love? Since when?'

'I don't know if he is in love with me, but I am. I have always been, from the first time I met him back home, when we were in school,' she reminisced.

I was baffled. Why then did she set him up for me? I didn't have the courage to ask her that. Some questions are best left alone. They spare us the pain of learning unpalatable truths about us, about those we love and pretend to love.

Juni crushed the empty plastic packet and tossed it into the bin in the corner. I was surprised to see an air of easy delight in her manner. If I were her, I would have been considering about the only choice open to me-suicide. Her eyes reflected a different intention though, a resolve that seemed distanced from my sinister consideration of ending life.

The fact that she had a husband who was bound to the bed back home, his family who tended to him, and above all, three sons over ten years of age didn't seem to cross her mind at all.

'So, what now?' I asked, again.

'I want to keep this baby.'

I grabbed Juni's hand. 'You must be joking!'

'I am not. I am going to deliver this baby. And you will help me in this.'

'Me?' The muscles in my neck began to get tense and I gave off a shudder. I clutched at the bedspread.

Juni's voice became tender as she took both my hands in hers. 'Don't you keep telling me that you can never thank me enough for all that I have done for you? That you will never find a way to repay me?'

I kept listening, fear gripping every cell in my structure. What was she arriving at? Why was she dragging me into all these? What's my role in this whole shambolic going to be?

Outside our room, we heard the door-bell ring. A food delivery boy, I thought, over my creeping unease. The door to our room was slightly ajar. We waited for the visitor to leave before speaking again. I felt as if we were discussing a conspiracy. My hands got clammy in Juni's gentle grip and I loosened myself out of it.

'Listen. I want this baby and I will do whatever it takes to keep it,' Juni said. The certitude in her voice amazed me first, and then alarmed me.

'But how?'

'We will move out of here. You and I. We will take a separate outhouse somewhere away from here, where no one would know us.'

I gulped, afraid to even give her a consenting nod. She was getting very daring and I wasn't certain that I wanted to be a part of her adventure. But there was nothing I could say. I owed so much to her.

'I have a friend who is a nurse. She will help me through my pregnancy and delivery at home. I have a contact in Manila whose help I will seek for making the baby's passport. I may have to pay heftily, but I am certain it will be done. I will go and get the passport after the baby is born. You will look after the baby till I return, won't you?'

The very idea was frightening. But Juni's mind was made up.

'Hmm...' I grunted softly, as if to acknowledge her decision. 'What does Joshua say?'

'Leave him out. He is not part of the story anymore.

This baby is just mine.' After a moment's silence she said dismissively, 'In any case, I wasn't expecting him to accept us into his life.'

She spoke as if it was a given that Joshua wanted no baggage on his back and curiously, she had no qualms about it. She was resigned to it.

The urine test confirmed Juni's pregnancy and soon we were making plans to move out. That evening I spoke to my parents and my children. They had already drawn up a list of things I must take for them, although my visit home was still a long way off. Dad and Mom said they could see the pictures I shared with them very well, now that the cataract was removed. They could do with a new pair of frames though, they added.

There was a general sense of contentment in their lives. It only reaffirmed my obligation towards Juni to be a partner in her plan. It wasn't like she was planning a murder, I argued with my feeble fears. All she wanted was to bring her child into this world. How could she help it if the law of this land didn't allow us to have children out of the wedlock?

Night after night, I imagined that all of what Juni had said to me were flashes of a nightmare, and I would wake up to know none of it was true. There were times when I secretly wished she would have a miscarriage. But Juni's growing baby bump quelled all my imagination and my dread grew as months passed.

The nurse who came to check on her periodically was a trained mid-wife back in the Philippines. I admired Juni's capacity for having the right kind of acquaintances to sort her problems. Maria here, the government official in Manila, and above all, me.

My anxiety peaked as time passed and Juni inched closer to her due date. She had not been going to work for several months now, and our house ran on her savings and my salary. It was beginning to pinch me hard, but then again, I had no way to walk away from what I had committed to Juni. Not now.

One night, just before dinner, Juni's water broke. 'Call Maria,' she instructed me. The calm on Juni's

face put all my incipient panic at rest. I wondered where Juni had summoned such courage from, what had given her the strength to face such adversities. God, I concluded, and touched my cross pendant with a solemn acknowledgment and prayer.

Maria arrived in fifteen minutes and took charge of the proceedings. It was as if everything was meticulously planned by them and all they had to do was to follow it. As I watched, Juni's love child was born and its fresh cry filled the room. I witnessed the magic of a new life coming into this world, yet again. Just that, this time, it wasn't from my belly. Something about Juni's love child made me feel as elated as I had felt when my own children were born.

Maria handed the baby to Juni who planted her first kiss on his forehead. How sacred that moment of first contact between the mother's quivering lips and the baby's supple skin was!

'He is a special child,' said Maria as she took the baby back to clean him. She sounded more sombre than the occasion had warranted and slightly nervous too.

I walked over to Maria, who by then had handed the baby back to Juni for his first feed. There was something unsettling about what I saw in Maria's eyes as she dropped her eyelids and turned away. What did her eyes convey? Apology? Sadness? Regret?

I went around and faced her. 'What is it?'

'I suspect Down Syndrome.' Her voice broke as she said it.

'Ah!' I threw my head up, closed my eyes.

I knew what it meant. My eyes flew frantically to the infant's face, and scanned for signs of what Maria had just declared. Although Maria had uttered the words softly to keep Juni out of earshot, Juni had heard it, nevertheless, and I saw tears begin to trickle from the corner of her eyes. She held her baby close to her breasts and rocked her body gently back and forth as if to reassure, both herself and the little thing. What thoughts must have rammed her head in that instant I cannot say, but this much I knew. Maria's troubles had just increased.

I walked up to the baby instinctively, touched the infant fingers and waited for them to clutch at mine. At the contact, I felt the love of the universe flow between us. And at the same time, I heard my heart crumble inside. As much as I wanted to wish it away, the truth remained. Juni's love child has flattened features and his eyes slanted upwards. He may not talk, laugh or do things like Joie, Chris or Sammy.

My head reeled and I felt an urgent need to talk to my children. I hurried out of the house and standing in the compound, I wept hard before calling them.

Chris was out in the yard playing. Joie said he missed me and cried. Sammy told me about his scraped knee from a recent fall. As I disconnected the call, I heard the crooning of a pigeon from below the air conditioner. Broken shells from an egg lay scattered below. There was one more egg waiting to hatch on top of the unit. The mother pigeon strutted impatiently around it after giving it the incipient warmth of life. Her anxiety was apparent even in the waning day light.

Two months after Juni's baby was born, I suggested that she must consider going back to our home country where she could raise the child without fear and with freedom.

'How will you keep him here without a visa?' I asked, and added cautiously, 'and he has a genetic disorder. You may not be able to deal with it, atey.' My voice wasn't devoid of compassion, but it was firm. I didn't mean to hurt Juni, but she had to take hard decisions.

'How do you suggest I smuggle him out of this place?' Juni cracked a faint smile lined with excruciating heartache.

She knew as much as I did that we were now stuck. The baby had no resident permit. He had no access to hospitals and doctors. Above all, he had special needs. Money was in shortage. Even the additional income from nights with rich men would be insufficient.

'The first thing I must do is to get him a passport. I am planning to go home for a week. I will then wait for the annual amnesty here and get ourselves deported. I can't think of a better way.' Juni shook her head in despair.

It wasn't a shoddy idea but what it implied was that Juni's baby will be under my care while she was away. A week wasn't a long time, but a baby only a few months old was a huge responsibility.

'I am nervous, Atey,' I said, wondering if I had a way to escape the ordeal. Didn't she really know how frightened I was of the mere prospect of it? Did she believe that I owed her so much that I could not say 'no' to this difficult demand? Could debts in life become so overwhelming? I felt as if I was caught in a cleft stick.

Juni booked to fly home a month later. The day of her departure was fraught with silent apprehension. Juni packed a few things for her family. I couldn't help but wonder if she would tell them about the baby.

There was a light rain as we took the taxi to the airport, and the sky was gathering more clouds.

'There has been a lot of rain this year,' I quipped just to lighten the mood.

'Artifical rain,' said Juni, implying cloud-seeding. It was funny that we were talking of weather to mask our uneasiness.

As soon as I sat in the taxi, to my utter surprise, Juni put the baby in my lap.

'For a week now, you will be his mom,' she squeezed my shoulder as if seeking my assurance.

I looked at the baby in deep slumber, oblivious to the predicament his life had caused. It was not his fault, but the fact that he had to endure the fallout of the circumstances in which he was born depressed me.

At the departure gate, Juni took the baby from me and a sob that was lurking inside, pushed passed its restrain and escaped her throat. I looked away unable to bear Juni's emerging pain. It was not just about parting with her son, but a lot more that words couldn't express at once.

She returned the baby to me, stood for a tentative moment as if she had something to say. And then, taking a deep breath, she turned around and walked away. I waited for her to wave before disappearing from sight, but she kept walking without looking back. In that moment, I felt a stir against my breast. The baby was awake and kicking my chest with his tiny feet. I felt he was knocking at my heart and seeking a place in my life. I hailed a taxi and placed the baby in the middle of the back seat. As I slid in and put him in my lap, my cell phone beeped.

'I am thinking of calling him Santos. Do you like the name?' the message read.

'Yes, it is lovely,' I replied. It had never occurred to me that Juni had not named the baby yet.

'He will be hungry when he wakes up. Have you taken the milk? Please take care of him till I return.'

'I sure will.'

'Tell Santos that his Mamma loves him. Despite everything.'

'Santos,' I whispered.

Santos gurgled. There was mystery in his baby eyes.

'Mamma loves you. Despite everything.'

CHAPTER ELEVEN

TWILIGHT

My name is Murthy. I have stopped putting a figure to my age because it doesn't matter anymore, neither to me nor to those around me. I only know that I am in that phase of life where there is very little to look forward to, and much to turn around and watch in retrospect with detachment.

I am now marching in the twilight zone, as a unit of the retreating army, watching and waiting for the sun to set on my life. Death. It is the only defining event left to happen in my life. It would be a welcome withdrawal, in many senses.

In fact, that is all that is left to happen in the lives of many like me.

I was witness to one such retreat last week.

Chellama's.

The only fleeting thought that passed my mind when I stood watching her motionless body was that I should have been lying there in her place. I strongly think that I am more eligible to move into the next realm than Chellama. After all, she still has a connection in the world—Mani, her half blind husband—while I virtually have none and my going away would affect nobody.

However, the rules of the game don't work that way; the roll call from above has no distinct order. To the distress of all those in the queue, it comes at random, taking away the less prepared ones earlier than those aching to go away. Chellama's death was proof to this phenomenon, and many of us were annoyed at her for jumping the line ahead of others here.

Her sudden exit has now left Mani rudderless in an existence that even otherwise had no direction, much like the rest of us here. A week has passed and he hasn't stopped grieving. He moans and wails in sorrow, to the discomfort of many among us. His explicit manner of mourning his wife's death overwhelms us and we take turns to counsel and sometimes to even chide him in utter despair.

'What do you think the rest of us here are doing with our lives? It is long since we lost any purpose or meaning. You are not the only one. So, stop grieving.' I said to him, gravely. I was still angry with Chellama for having beaten me to death.

I didn't mean to be poignant, rude, or apologetic about our geriatric state, but I had wanted him to acknowledge the fact that we were all much like him. None of us had any constructive business in life anymore. In fact, he has been fortunate to have Chellama this far, holding his hand, leading him in his world of semi darkness, and keeping him from faltering at the steps, while the rest of us only had assorted memories of spouses and families. And memories of such varied kind they are!

'She has found her shore. Now it is upon you to row the boat and reach the other side of life,' I said, as Mani whimpered and then slowly fell silent.

He wasn't alone, I averred, he had twelve others 'single digit human beings' (as I described our kind of people), for company and the thirteenth would soon occupy Chellama's vacant place.

'We don't have much distance to cover in any case,' I said after a long pause, almost irrelevantly, putting my hand on his shoulder and looking tenderly into his tear- softened eyes.

As I said that, I had a picture of an old, withered flock walking towards the horizon in my mind: a collective march towards the final frontier.

I must have appeared only as a blur to Mani given his lack of sight, but he knew what I meant and nodded thoughtfully. He held the hand that I offered and began to weep bitterly once again, and I felt that he was crying for all of us. We old folks make a curious spectacle when we cry and for some reason, we don't get laughed at for it. If anything, we get a few fleeting words of sympathy. There are many things other than pity that we so deserve.

Now, Chellama.

It is true that her absence would be felt by us very deeply, not just because she was the only woman in our midst, but also because she was the chattiest among us. She was our mother, sister, and daughter, all rolled into one. She cobbled up a family of old persons from a bunch of infirm, disheartened castaways. She was like the elastic band that held grey, lifeless hair strands together. I remember the first time I met the couple—Mani and Chellama. It was soon after my admission into this place by my daughter and son-in-law two years ago.

It was my first day away from home.

It is not easy to express the anguish felt by an old person being led into the porch of a place like this. The heart, mind, and body are in convulsion, and it is difficult to know if it is resentment, sorrow, fear, or a confluence of all of them that makes the limbs tremble.

'Where are you taking grandpa?' My eight-year-old grandson asked his parents, as we prepared to leave the house.

I waited for the answer, if only to know what they thought about it. They certainly must have thought of a story to tell the little one. Children these days demand explanation for adult behaviour in a manner our generation never contemplated.

'To the boarding,' said my son-in-law, tucking Vicky's shirt into his shorts.

Boarding. I thought it was a clever reply.

'But why does he have to go to the boarding?'

'Because he can't stay with us. Daddy and mummy go to work and there is no one to take care of him at home. What if he falls and hurts himself while we are all away?'

Now, that is a statement of concern, unmistakably, but with so much of travesty. Or was I being merely sceptical?

'But he hasn't fallen even once. You won't fall either, will you grandpa?'

'I may. I am old,' I said. What more could I have said to him? It was true that with my weakening spine and wobbly limbs, I could have tripped over even a paper cup and who after all could bear the consequences of doctor, medicine, tending?

'Who will take care of you in the boarding?' Vicky asked trying to understand the situation.

'There are many people,' I said drawing him close to me and watching his eyelids flutter with doubt. He somehow didn't seem convinced and I could see it from his cherubic face.

'Will you have friends there?'

'Maybe, I think I will.' I did not want to disappoint him.

I did not know what to expect in my boarding: happiness and friendship or desolation and acrimony. Strangely, I did not have any reason to expect anything better than what I was already enduring with my family. The world outside didn't have an obligation to be fair or better either. I have always had that much consideration for the world and its people.

'And TV to watch cartoon?' my grandson asked eagerly breaking into my thoughts.

At his age, friends and cartoons are significant considerations. I thought that a reply in the affirmative would comfort him as much as he thought it would enliven my days.

Vicky and I often watched cartoons together, although in the beginning I had little interest in the noisy, colour-washed series that made sense only to him. In the years following my retirement and then the death of my wife Lakshmi, I had taken to spirituality. Not in the sublime sense that one talks about it, but in the mundane level where in a person keeps himself preoccupied with religious activities like chanting verses or reading mythology. This was soon replaced with the time Vicky and I spent together. It gave us both a sense of belongingness to each other and made me an audience to the cartoons whenever he chose to, which was far more frequent than what his parents would have liked. I learned to enjoy the animated moments on TV along with him, and those moments became my only incentive in life.

Now, they were robbing me of the sole source of joy in my life and I didn't make even a feeble protest. I was acting as though it didn't make a difference, or didn't it really make a difference?

'Grandpa, let us know if you have TV in your boarding or else Daddy will buy you one,' Vicky said.

His innocence touched me, and I wondered whatever happened to such naiveté when children grew into adults and from where they imbibed the apathy and brashness that had become the hallmarks of the new age adults.

'But it would be so boring without you for company,' I said fondly, raising my hand to stroke his head, but not quite doing it for some reason.

'Yeah, it would be boring for me too,' he acknowledged thoughtfully, perhaps not knowing what else to say.

I was glad that Vicky was accepting my going away with such equanimity or it would have made my departure such a melodramatic event.

I marvelled at the new generation: wise, picking up quick lessons in adaptability and acceptance, making room for changes in their life, and putting old things behind them and moving on. I saw myself taking a leaf out of this new age approach when I took leave of them to walk after the attendant to the dormitory that would be my shelter for the rest of my life.

Although I paused for a moment before turning in, I did not turn around for the last wave. It was just a wry, cold occasion to 'let go' of the past and I decided not to lug any emotional baggage from there into my future life (or whatever was left of it).

As soon as the attendant left after showing me my cot—a steel one, painted green—my new relations closed in, eager to introduce and get to know. They all seemed equally apprehensive about the arrival of a new bird into their nest and it was Chellama who first broke the silence.

'The manager had informed us about your coming and we have all been waiting since morning,' she said.

I was pleased that the world still had people who waited for me. People who I did not even remotely know. It was a strange feeling and the beginning of a new way of spending life.

'Murthy, isn't it?' Chellama asked. I nodded.

'Since you look older than most of us here, I think we will all call you Murthy mama. What do you say?' she asked the others in the dorm. It appeared no one refuted anything that Chellama said in the dorm.

Then she proceeded to introduce the rest of them. She gave a brief about each, and in the days that followed, I was amused at the ease with which she described their personal history, replete with tales of geriatric angst. It was as though she were emptying a rucksack full of collective memories, sorting and attaching them to names in the dorm. And she did it with such an air of detachment that the men around her listened to their stories once again with a calm disposition, as though it never belonged to them.

She would prod them now and again to help her with the details, saying, 'Gopi anna, why don't you tell Murthy mama how your wife once walked out of home when you emptied the food into the garbage bin merely because it had a tinge of extra salt? And how you waited for her to return from her home for a week before you went and fetched her yourself.'

Gopinathan, who hailed from Kerala, would then grin at the thought and shake his head remembering his wife.

'That was the first time I realised what it is like to live without her. It wasn't easy. I had then made her promise that she would never walk out on me again. But she did not keep the promise, she did go away after all,' he would say slipping into a sullen mood.

We all nodded with him, thinking our own sombre thoughts.

'And Murthy mama, did you know that when Pachu anna's daughter-in-law got so fed up with his singing

talents that she brought him here? He must have been such a bother for them to do it, eh?' Chellama would then pick on Pachu or Parasuraman from Madras some more. 'I was a good singer, giving lessons to dozens of children even after I retired from service. I can't help if people don't develop tastes,' Pachu anna would say in his defence. 'I still have such good control over my vocal cords,' he would claim touching the shrivelled skin on his throat gently.

'Yes, of course. Don't we know all know about it?' Chellama would say sniggering behind her palm and break into a folk song that briefly transported us out of the Home and into the fields in a far-flung village in Tamil Nadu.

Taking cue, Parasuraman would then take off to the rhythmic clap of our hands and we would soon have a concert.

Chellama was very sprightly for her age. She liked to be the matron in the dorm and went about supervising our lives with maternal care and youthful alacrity. We had a tacit tolerance for her excesses, which ranged from her incessant babble to the perennial TV watching tendency to screaming the life out of her reticent husband. She had indeed grown tired of being his attendant, and she made it known frequently.

'When will you ever give me some peace, old man? Wish I could dump you somewhere just as your children did,' she would yell unkindly. When Mani asked her for water while she watched her TV serials, she would keep her attention fixed to the screen.

Mani would merely gaze straight through his half blind eyes. He had become what I referred to as a 'habitual dependent'. He would wait for the commercial break and then call out again. She would then throw a stare and fetch him a glass of water along with some complimentary mutterings. And to think that Mani mourned for such a grouchy old woman!

Yet she was his wife and the fact that she complimented his taciturn existence with her loud manner made Mani feel incomplete after her departure. It was as if his lightless life had also become a noiseless one; for the noises around him made by the rest of us had become almost inconsequential. It was as though his existence had hinged on the dual aspect of Chellama, brash yet doggedly caring about her husband. For no matter how much she ranted at him, she always realised that together they made a world of their own. It was evident from the manner in which she took him by hand to the dining hall, handed him his tablets, waited for him to sleep before she went to sleep and checked on him every once in a while, during the night.

It was an amusing yet touching ritual.

I had once caught Chellama's shadowy figure approach Mani's cot and watch him silently. The night lamp in the dorm was diffused enough to induce sleep, but it was also bright enough to reveal Chellama's stealthy movement in sharp relief. She gently wiped the sweat off Mani's brow, fanned him for a few lasting moments with the free end of her saree and before leaving, put her hand on his chest and her fingers below his nostrils as though to make sure that he was breathing. Since some days, she seemed to be seized by a sense of foreboding that suddenly emerged in the haze of the night.

On nights when the fluttering noise of Mani's snore did not rend the air, she would sneak up to his cot, put her hand to his chest and then watch him for a while as though to convey her deepest fears to her sleeping husband.

And so, night after night, I waited for Mani to sleep and begin snoring and when he did not, I waited for Chellama to come up and confirm his well-being, ascertain that he had not quit her life without notice. On many nights, I have had to restrain myself from asking her aloud, 'Is he alive?'

It was odd that Chellama's fear of Mani dying in his sleep had infected me as well. It was as though on one of those nights, Chellama would suddenly find Mani's heart stopped forever.

It was a secret fear that Chellama, and I on her behalf, harboured. I tried to find traces of it in her eyes during the day but was surprised to see her display none of it amidst her daylong activities in the dorm and out of it.

I know very little about Mani and Chellama, for she rarely spoke about their past, and not being too inquisitive about other people's lives, I never tried to know much about them or the others. I could gather that Chellama broke her life into little portions of laughter, fear, sadness, care, and anger. She allocated specific time, and thought to each, not allowing one to intercept the other. She was a peculiar person with neatly structured emotions. And her going away has left an inexplicable sense of loss and emptiness in our lives. We did not mourn her passing, but we began to miss her presence in our midst.

It is like missing the rains after a nagging monsoon season.

In my estimation, things would not have changed had the couple not returned to their son's home last December. They had not gone on their own volition. The day Chellama received the letter from her son, she was grave and morose. It was not only Mani who bore the brunt of her wrath. She spewed her anger at all who met her that day.

We rarely received letters from our people. There is some correspondence in the first few months after coming here, which slowly dwindles and then stops altogether. By then, it really would not matter for us as for those who sent them. So, the arrival of a letter for Chellama sparked off speculation amongst us—was anyone ill in the family? Was there a grandson or granddaughter born? Was anyone getting married?

Chellama's first reaction to the news of the letter was a confluence of surprise, despise, and thrill, and there was no way of knowing which of them gained primacy in her heart in that spilt moment.

'Letter for us?' she turned from the TV screen to ask the manager.

'Yes, from your son.'

'From Raja?' She gasped with uncertain anticipation.

I could see that it was a gasp of delight. It came with such suddenness that it made her joy more obvious than she had wanted it to be. Then within a moment, the joy turned to a wry sentiment.

'What does he want now from these useless lives?' She unknotted her hair resting at the back of her neck and tied it up once again. 'Wait until this episode ends,' she said casually, as though the serial on TV was paramount than the letter. As the manager turned to go, she said, 'No, wait. I will go with you. God knows what it is.'

All said and done, it is hard for us to desist from relationships. Harder still to resist the subtle expressions of it.

Chellama rose from the floor in front of the TV and said to Mani as she went past his cot, 'Your son has sent a letter, it seems. Let me go and find out what it is about.' None of us in the dorm could miss the resentment in her voice. We waited for her to return from the office room.

Gopinathan seized the opportunity to turn the volume of the TV down, giving us all a much-needed respite. I went back to my religious reading. The calm in the dorm was laced with a sense of impatience and anxiety, and I could feel an air of collective restiveness pervade the place. The summer heat that came down the asbestos roof made our waiting for Chellama more agonising and a few old feet strayed out of the dorm, more as an escape from the disquiet than with any specific purpose.

My limbs have been weakening fast lately, and I went out only during the meal hours. I had begun to realise that my lower parts, waist downward, were slowly failing and the present wobble was a sign of a complete breakdown, sooner or later. With dread, I thought of a life struck by paralysis, immobile and unwanted.

I broke into cold sweat. Holding the religious text close to my chest I said a prayer for a swift, painless redemption.

Chellama returned from the office room looking more disconcerted than she had ever been in the past. We waited for her to tell us what good or bad news the letter had brought. But Chellama spoke nothing for a while.

'Your son wants us to go home,' she then said slowly, gently laying a hand on Mani's shoulder. 'He is coming to take us this week.'

Chellama had never been this distraught.

'Why? That is good news,' said Muthu from where he sat picking his ears. 'You are truly lucky.'

Chellama turned towards him, her face devoid of any emotion, and waved desultorily. We could not make anything of the gesture.

'Do you want to go?' she asked Mani who had his eyes fixed somewhere past Chellama.

'Do you? We will go if you wish to,' said Mani.

'I don't, but how do we say no to him?'

'Turn him away when he comes.' Mani flicked the air frantically.

Chellama shook her head. She knew that there was no escape. They will have to go. They had long since lost the privilege to make decisions about their lives. Whoever said that old age is childhood revisited, said it right. It is a period in life when you always have people around to make decisions for you and push you around. Your only choice was to comply without tantrums.

We watched the couple as they sat in silence, contemplating their life ahead.

It is funny but true that after a while at the Home, we prefer not to be dragged back into the drudgery of the world outside. We are fearful of losing our peace, of breaking the delicate balance our lives have attained and we are loath to give up the modest freedom that we enjoyed here.

Mani and Chellama spent the next three days contemplating about an undesired family reunion. It was the only time Chellama spoke about her family, and we listened with sympathy, even as some of us drew parallels and some others were glad to have been spared similar ordeals.

'She has got a job,' said Chellama, referring to her daughter-in-law. 'The children are at home and it would cost a lot to employ someone to look after them. He is right...he is right. There is no need to spend money on someone from outside while we are still alive.'

It was as though she was speaking to herself, trying to reconcile.

'Do you think they will be happy?' asked Gopinathan to me that evening. 'I wouldn't be if I were in their place. It can never again be the same. Never.' He was categorical about it.

I said nothing. I tried not to think about what I would do if I were in their place.

I was glad that my daughter and her husband had relocated to Canada. Nobody would come to take me on a vacation from the Home.

Three days later Mani and Chellama's son, Raja, came to fetch them.

'I am glad that you are taking them home. They need your care and affection at this stage. No matter how hard we try, we cannot be their family. They are lucky to have you as son,' the manager spoke words of gentle appreciation. I wondered if he had rehearsed the lines over the past two days or if he had stocked statements to say in specific situations.

'It wasn't out of choice that we brought them here. Just circumstances. But now I want them back. Thank you for all that you have done,' Raja said.

Before leaving, Chellama walked up to us with Mani, helped him to shake hand with each of us, and left without a parting word.

The storm in our dorm walked out of the compound with her shadow in tow. The TV took a sabbatical for two days after the departure of Mani and Chellama. Then Gopinathan said that life in the dorm was losing its intrinsic quality without the blare from the box.

'We need some noise in here,' he declared and turned it on.

'I don't think we really need it. Not at this noon hour. We would do better to take a nap,' I said, irritated at being robbed off my siesta.

'Why, we all slept even while the TV was on earlier,' he said.

'Put the news on then,' I said.

'No, let the Sunday movie play. What are we going to do knowing who killed whom and where or what the government does or not?' said Easwaran grimly, as he sat up from his recline.

I threw a loathsome glance at him and thought, your craving for the trivial hasn't gone yet. Does it become your age to watch women swaying their hips to lilting tunes with disgusting lyrics?

I was pleased that I didn't say the words aloud. It could have led to an unnecessary spat; one that our dorm hadn't witnessed while Chellama was still around watching endless serials on the TV. I was surprised that in her presence we never had differences. We never thought of questioning her love for the televised drama even when it disturbed our sleep or pierced our ears.

Our tolerance somehow seemed to wilt in Chellama's absence.

It is curious how a stranger can turn an assorted cluster into a harmonised unit. Some people, I reckoned, had the ability to lend a magical touch to other's lives, even when they seemed rough from the outside. That way, Chellama's unrefined manner had a unique charm, which we began to miss immensely, and watching TV was only one of the many ways we found to make her absence felt less.

Another day of void dawned in our nowhere-to-go,nothing-much-to-do lives.

I stretched my legs, felt the pain along their length, and groaned under my breath. I wished I could give out a long wail. Random thoughts clouded my mind.

I thought of Vicky. I thought of Mani and Chellama.

Then I thought of my death.

Eventually, whoever thought of Mani and Chellama as fortunate to be reunited with their family was proved wrong. Surprise of surprises, we had the couple trudging in oncc again to the dorm four months after they had left us.

'We are glad to receive you once again. But it is unfortunate that you had to return,' the manager said, taking Mani's hand.

'We have nowhere else to go and we were certain that you will not turn us away,' said Chellama.

She seemed to have lost all her sprightliness. Pale and downcast, she was a picture of fatigue as though she had been through tough, turbulent times.

'You are lucky that your beds are still unoccupied. We have had many enquiries and we were on the verge of taking two men in place of you two.'

Chellama smiled weakly, almost meaning to say,

'Thank you.'

Where would they have gone had the vacancies been filled? I wondered.

'I don't believe that Raja has put them back here

again. Wonder what went wrong,' said Easwaran.

'Going back home. That is what was wrong,' I said, indignantly.

I felt the pain shoot down from my back to the end of my limbs. I leaned on Easwaran and tried to steady my stance. Someday soon, I will collapse like a decrepit building, I thought.

Why had Raja taken them if only he had to get them back here again? Were we, the old tribe, so obscenely dispensable to them?

'It is good that they are back,' said Viswam, 'but bad that they had to.'

We all nodded at once and unanimously decided that we would not probe them about it. We were eager to share their pain, but wary of worsening it by asking. Knowing Chellama, we were certain that she would spill the truth sooner or later.

For days Chellama spoke nothing. She was morose, and went about her routine, tending to Mani, attending to his frequent calls without a protest, and watching TV without the usual display of interest.

And one day amidst the silence, she left us forever. I remember that she had not checked on Mani that night and I had waited till past midnight before falling asleep. It had never crossed my mind at that moment that Chellama herself had rested, forever.

We were surprised that her son did not come to claim her body. She was given a humble farewell in keeping with the norms of the Home. The absence of her family was glaring, but that was what she had desired for them. 'They did not want their family to know if they died,' said the manager. 'There were problems between them.' 'That's probably why Raja left them back here,'

Viswam said the obvious.

'No, he didn't send them back here. They came of their own. This time they discarded their son.'

We nodded, pensively, partly with sympathy and partly with sadness.

'It was a good thing to do, walking out on him for once. What do you say?' Swamy asked me abruptly as we returned to our private shells.

'Yes, it was,' I said, stretching myself to rest.

CHAPTER TWELVE

THE END

'Do you...regret it?'

I did not know what to make of Dad's question. From the way he asked it—feeble and tentative—I could see he was a broken man just about completing a ritual of living his time out. He had insisted on coming to the courtroom on the last day of hearing but I didn't want him to witness the inevitable in person. I stopped him from coming by taking Mom's alibi. 'You must be with her now rather than me.'

As soon as the procedural formalities were over, I called him and suggested we go out for a coffee. I didn't want to go home straight. Trying to normalize the atmosphere as if nothing had happened would only be a travesty of sorts and I needed some time to gather myself before I went home and pacified Mom.

'Do you?' he asked again.

I looked him in the eye and smiled, smugly.

'Excuse me,' I said, alerting a waiter. 'Please take this coffee away and bring me another one without a damned frothy heart. What makes your company think that all the people who walk in here are hopelessly in love? How insensitive can you guys get, eh?' I barked.

I knew I was being unreasonable with him, but I had to vent my ire somewhere. The love motifs around me on the occasion of Valentine's Day were the most morbid reminders of my past. They filled me with despise of the kind that I had never felt before. But...I must find my calm now. I had an entire lifetime to spew venom on the world that had peeled the last shred of romantic sentiments off me.

The world? Not quite. Who then was responsible for the mess that I was in? I felt like a mop of tousled hair, knotted from all ends.

I pushed up my specs towards the brows and pressed my eyes to squeeze the fatigue out. Where had all the dampness in them gone, I wondered. I couldn't have spent it on a frigging man who didn't know the difference between a wife and a whore. Or did I?

'Regret what, Dad? The marriage, the divorce or three years of my putting up with the sham?' I asked, careful not to show disdain.

I knew it was harsh, but it was something I had been asking myself repeatedly. Which part of my life did I regret, and which part of it was I guilty of surrendering without defence? Which decisions of mine were ridiculous or which ones were insane? When did I hand in the reins and when did I realise it was time to reclaim it all?

As I waited for Dad to answer, the waiter brought my coffee, and asked deferentially, 'Is this okay, ma'am?'

There was still too much froth on the surface, too visually cloying, but it wasn't as offensive as before. Even a coffee laved in the love sign seemed vulgar to me. 'Marriage is a ghastly thing, isn't it? Or is it love that is ghastlier?' I asked blowing into the coffee.

Two heart-shaped balloons burst somewhere at the back of the coffee shop where two children were thumping the balloons in the air. Then two more followed.

'Funny!' I scoffed. How much more perverse and preposterous can this day and moment get? Hearts popping all around me on a day the judge ruled that my marriage had officially ended. That love can now take a hike in my life.

'Say something, Dad,' I coaxed him to speak. 'What am I supposed to regret? You and mom have always guided me, told me what to do and what not to. You made sure that I was a good daughter, towed the line and kept your honour. I didn't do anything wrong, did I? So, what do I have to regret exactly? It was all hunky-dory. Of course, barring what happened today. That was not in your script, was it? I am sorry to disappoint you and Mom.'

I had my first sip of the coffee without sugar. I did it deliberately, just to challenge my taste buds but the nasty little things would have none of it and demanded that I give them their due.

'Coffee without sugar is on par with freshly brewed poison,' Satish would say. It was also his favourite metaphor, given that I was called Cheeni at home. He was the coffee and I was the sugar. I always teased him for the mushiness in the metaphor, but he revelled in it.

It was he who had permanently turned my chaste coffee to a cloying syrup. What queer habits that naughty elf had put in me! From slurping over-sweet coffee to guzzling draught beer to running with the waves to singing 90's karaoke in the weekends.

My fingers hovered over the sugar sachets, remembering him, unable to decide between the brown and white versions. I took three of each.

Dad, all the while, watched me silently. His coffee remained untouched. I could say by his solemn looks that he was brimming with emotions, none of which he could articulate. The torture of having to bear a sentiment that struggles to find expression is all too familiar to me. I couldn't blame him. It was a most extraordinary situation. Finding words to say to a freshly divorced daughter isn't easy.

What could he say, after all? That I would find my match again from the hundreds of men that I will meet in my life. That everything will be back in the groove soon? Or that he was devastated to see me shelved and severed from domesticity like an over-used floor mop? Or that he worried what people might now speak about our family? About how they would judge him and his wife, and therefore I must not let anyone get wind of it at once?

I hadn't the faintest clue about what was running in his mind in that moment.

'Have your coffee, Dad. It is no good if it isn't hot.

Shall I ask her to warm it?'

Dad declined the offer to reheat it and took a few quick sips. He did the right thing. Coffee shouldn't be reheated. It would lose its innate flavour and the deep spiritual experience it brings to our South Indian palates.

Once cold, it only deserved damnation.

It was not my contention. It was one of Satish's original coffee sutras. The rogue had such unique ways to charm people! There was never a dull moment in life when he was around. Why didn't he appeal to Dad and Mom then?

I still refuse to believe that it was the caste crap that came between us. If I had the slightest inkling that my parents cared so much for the class and religion thing, I would never have disclosed our affair to them. I would have silently married him without much fuss. It was easily doable, and if I didn't adopt that route, it was only because I had unfailing faith in them. Not for once, did I suspect that they would have objections, that they would not accept Satish whole-heartedly. I had naively thought that my parents had evolved in their beliefs and would stand by their child through thick and think.

They had always been moderate, sometimes even modern, in their views. I was rarely put in shackles and was given permission to make my own career choices. Then again, marriage is an entirely different thing. It turns all previously held principles on their head. It makes a mockery of modernity and exposes the real philosophies that one actually holds.

Satish fell outside the purview of their modern thinking and they refused to give us their blessings.

How I loathe that day of shameless showdown at home over our relationship! Mom went to the extent of threatening us with dire consequences should we arbitrarily decide to defy them. I might have had the guts to walk out of home but I didn't have the courage to take Mom's threat lightly.

'She is capable of doing it,' I said to Satish, when I met him the next day.

'What other option do we have?' he asked looking at the distance.

'Not many, I am afraid,' I said looking in the same direction as him.

'So?'

'So, nothing,' I shrugged.

Satish knitted his brows and thrust his head forward as if to ask if I had meant what he had assumed my 'nothing' meant.

'What else do you expect me to do?'

'Wait, perhaps, for them to get used to the idea.'

'Caste and religious differences are old ideas, Satish. It is like fish scent. Inseparable from those who have made it their creed. It has nothing to do with the progressive posture one puts up on the outside by their clothes and manner. I wonder how I didn't anticipate it. I trusted them to give us their consent. I didn't have the smallest clue.'

The more I thought about it, the more I became baffled at their obstinate stance. Did it really matter to them that Satish was an orthodox Christian? Or was it the fact that he grew up in an orphanage that rankled them?

'What if you had known about their beliefs? Would it have changed anything between us?' Satish asked me.

I shook my head bleakly.

Four cups of coffee got cold and wasted that day. Little did I know that behind my back, Dad and Mom were arranging my alliance in stealth. How they managed to bring a proposal to fruition in two weeks is still beyond me. Even before Satish and I could weigh our options for charting a future together, they had made their plans and executed it.

How deftly parents use the weapon of emotional blackmail, don't they? The day I was supposed to be 'seen', I texted Satish and said, 'Forgive me for this betrayal. I am going to agree to whatever Dad and Mom say. Certainly not of my own volition but from where I am, I cannot see far into the distance. I am completely disoriented, and it is hard for me survive in this state for long.'

The reply I received will haunt me for the rest of my life. Satish wrote, 'Who are you betraying, after all? Me or yourself?'

Why do people give in? Even when we know the right from the not-right, why do we often choose the latter willingly? Even when we know the path to happiness, why do we steer ourselves towards heartache and misery? We dawdle between our Yes and No so much that we end up saying one for the other?

'Inhaling the rancid smell of an empty coffee cup is injurious to health.' Satish's voice rang in my ear. It felt so real that I looked around with a fleeting glance, not certain if I had wanted him to miraculously find him standing there. I asked the waiter to remove the empty cups.

Dad had been completely silent until then, only grunting and muttering small responses ever since we met outside the court after the proceedings. 'How did it go?' he asked in a small voice.

'As expected,' I simpered. Then waving desultorily, I asked, 'What does one expect from a man who accuses his wife of adultery to get rid of her? One who accused her of sleeping around with other men, called her a prostitute in front of the court only because she worked hard and earned more than him?'

Dad squeezed my shoulder at the mention of the unmentionable P word. For a passing moment, I regretted having uttered it. I put myself in his place and felt the emotions roiling in his heart. There was a raging storm inside, rocking his boat hither and tither, sensing that he was far from the coast and might be at sea for a long time now. He maintained calm, although. He probably knew that he had to be my anchor now, more than ever before. Regardless of all his previous duplicity. Despite his faulty decisions in the past.

'It's over. It's all over. There's more life ahead of you. Now you must work on erasing the past and start afresh.' Erase the past? How preposterous! This was exactly what he had said to me when I was denied my love and was asked to forgo Satish; when I supplicated in front of them to let me live my life; when a stranger encroached on my heart to try and fill Satish's place.

What a travesty of an advice, Dad, I quietly thought.

The waiter brought the check and Dad opened his wallet.

'Dad, I will pay. This is my break-up treat to you,' I said. I was happy that he didn't notice the pungency in my voice.

'No, let me pay. Let me begin my atonement with this,' he said, placing his card inside the check jacket. 'For three days now, I have been thinking of this moment. With dread, I must say. This moment when I would come face to face with you after it's all over. I don't know what I must say to you, what is appropriate. I guess there is nothing much I can say except I am sorry. Forgive me, daughter, for dragging you through all this.'

Dad was on the brink of breaking down. His face was stretched taut and could have ripped at the corners any moment. I could see that it had taken a lot of effort for him to say those words. That explained the long silence that preceded his admission. He was perhaps gathering the courage and strength to concede that he had failed his daughter, grossly.

No, I didn't want Dad to whimper in front of me. I didn't want him to look weak and pathetic. I didn't want him to live with the guilt of breaking my life.

'Will you forgive me? Please,' he asked again, his eyes now melting into copious tears.

'Dad,' I said and grabbed his hand. I wasn't prepared for this.

What does a daughter tell a father pleading for mercy? Especially when she acknowledged that his role in ruining her life has been substantial?

That she forgave him? It would be a lie, a discredit to her aching soul.

That she would hold a grudge against him for the rest of her life? What a sacrilege! She'd be dead before she spoke those words to someone who had denied her nothing in life, except the man she loved. How gross a transgression was it?

'My forgiveness is irrelevant, Dad,' I said patting his hand. 'You did what you deemed right at that point. It wasn't out of spite. Similarly, I don't believe what happened was right but that doesn't mean I don't love you any less. This pain is an interlude in my life, and I will tide over it. Trust me, I will.'

Dad nodded placidly, dabbing his eyes. 'I should have let you marry him,' he conceded, slowly. 'Where would he be now?'

'Who? Satish?' I cocked my head and squinted at him. 'No, you can't be thinking of that, Dad. It is ridiculous.' Before he could say anything further, I rose to my feet. 'Shall we? I have had four missed calls from Mom. She will be concerned.'

Seeing Dad struggle to get up, I gave him a hand, which he gratefully took and slid out of the seat. He smiled at me feebly and repeated, 'I am sorry.'

'Don't worry, Dad. There is only one way life can go from here. Forward.'

Before we walked out, I spotted the waiter standing next to the billing counter and I moved towards him.

'I'm sorry. I didn't mean to be harsh. It was a hard day.'

I didn't know what made me presume he had a girl in his life, but I nevertheless tucked some money into his pocket and said, 'Here, buy your girl some red roses. Happy Valentine's. And, be a knight. Make sure no one else gets her.'

'Yes, Ma'am. Happy Valentine's to you too,' he said, coyly.

I smiled, nodded, and whispered to myself, 'Yes, of course. Happy Valentine's to me!'

About The Author

Asha Iyer Kumar was born in Chennai, India and brought up in Kerala. She graduated in English Literature and did her master's in journalism from the university of Kerala. She relocated to the Middle East in 1998.

Her first novel came out in 2009 and she has published five more books since then—two collections of short stories, a collection of poetry, and a compilation of her columns written for UAE's popular daily, *Khaleej Times*, in her solo non-fiction title.

Her writing has an overarching theme of life's poignancy, and it finds ample expression in her short stories. Asha is a Children's Life-Writing Coach and Youth Motivating Speaker. She lives in Dubai with her husband. She has been a columnist, feature writer and editorial consultant with *Khaleej Times.*

That Pain in the Womb is her sixth book.

Her other books are as follows –

Hymns from the Heart (Poetry, 2015)
Let it be, Love (Short stories, 2018)
Life is an emoji (Collection of essays, 2020)
That Pain in the Womb (Short Stories, 2021)
Sandstorms, Summer Rains (Novel, 2022)

www.ingramcontent.com/pod-product-compliance
Lightning Source LLC
LaVergne TN
LVHW091330150826
845673LV00006B/1819

* 9 7 9 8 8 9 4 9 8 6 1 4 2 *